Skating on Thin Ice

(Seattle Sockeyes Hockey)

Game On in Seattle #1

BY JAMI DAVENPORT

Edited and Revised 2nd Edition

Cover by
Hot DAMN DESIGNS
www.HotDamnDesigns.com

This book is a work of fiction. While reference might be made to actual historical events or existing locations, the names, characters, places, and incidents are either the product of the author's imagination or are used fictitiously, and any resemblance to actual persons, living or dead, business establishments, events, or locales is entirely coincidental.

Email: jamidavenport@hotmail.com
Website: http://www.jamidavenport.com
Twitter: @jamidavenport
Facebook: http://www.facebook.com/jamidavenport
Fan Page: http://www.facebook.com/jamidavenportauthor

Sign up for Jami's Newsletter

He trusts his gut, she trusts her numbers, and neither trusts the other, as a billionaire's mission to bring hockey to Seattle clashes with his passion for the woman who holds his heart.

Ethan Parker, a billionaire determined to bring professional hockey to Seattle, will stop at nothing to realize his dream. After signing an agreement to purchase another city's team, Ethan is anxious to make the move to Seattle, but a gag order by the league forces him to keep the sale a secret until the season ends, leaving him no choice but to go undercover as a consultant to study his team during the playoffs.

Lauren Schneider, Assistant Director of Player Personnel for the Giants hockey team, gets no respect from the team's testosterone-loaded staff. When Ethan bursts onto the scene, full of charm and genuinely interested in her opinions, she shares the team's weaknesses and discovers a weakness of her own—for Ethan. But when his true identity is revealed, and he starts cleaning house based on her unwitting input, his betrayal cuts deeply on both a professional and personal level. Bound by an employment contract, Lauren reluctantly moves to Seattle to work for the newly christened Seattle Sockeyes and her sexy, infuriating boss.

Lauren and Ethan must come to terms with their passions—for the team, for hockey, and for each other. Will their situation build a frozen wall between them, or will their love burn hot enough to melt the ice shielding their hearts?

DEDICATION

For Patty, for the love of the game, this one's for you.

And to all those hockey fans in the Pacific Northwest waiting for those in power to do the right thing and give us a team.

Special thanks to Wade and Jessica, united through hockey and skating, the cutest couple ever.

AUTHOR'S NOTE

I'm so thrilled to introduce my new sports romance series, *Game On in Seattle*, which will include subseries for Seattle Sockeyes hockey, a Seattle baseball team, and a new Seattle football team.

It's never easy to leave the comfort of the known for the unknown. *Skating on Thin Ice* is my first foray into indie publishing. You'll notice some fun changes, such as old characters returning from previously published books. In the case of *Skating on Thin Ice*, Brad Reynolds, who first appeared in my *Evergreen Dynasty* series as the hero's brother, is Ethan's best friend.

I'm a huge Seattle sports fan, which comes as no surprise to those of you who've hung out on my Facebook or Twitter or read my former series. I've been crossing all my toes and fingers that Seattle will get a professional hockey team in the near future. Since as of this writing that hasn't happened yet, I decided to create that very scenario in my fictional world with the Seattle Sockeyes and give Seattle the hockey team the Pacific Northwest fans so deserve.

Chapter 1—The Penalty Box

Ethan Parker came into this world with a silver spoon in his mouth. He would've preferred a hockey stick in his hands, but sometimes those were the breaks.

He'd never skate in the pros or hoist the Stanley Cup in victory, but that didn't squelch his enthusiasm for everything hockey. Two to three times a week, he played for an adult league in a rink minutes south of Seattle, while he dreamed of one day bringing professional hockey to the Emerald City.

And maybe, just maybe, he'd realize that dream in the near future.

Months ago the Sleezer brothers—yes, seriously that was their name—contacted the Puget Sound Hockey Alliance through Ethan's attorney, Cyrus North, with an offer Ethan couldn't refuse, so he did what any billionaire with a hockey obsession would do—he wrote them a big check and waited.

And waited.

And waited.

Increasingly impatient, he slid a blank check for relocation fees under the table to the league and waited some more. Nothing happened. Not a damn thing. So much for money talking. His considerable bankroll wasn't even whispering to the hockey powers that be.

It'd been months since he'd heard a peep. While a day didn't go by that he didn't wonder what the hell was or wasn't happening, tonight *wasn't* about his frustrations with professional hockey. Tonight was all about immersing himself at the game's most basic level while getting down and dirty with his amateur teammates. Tonight was about playing the game he loved with a bunch of guys equally as rabid. And tonight reminded him of all the reasons why he couldn't give up until Seattle had a big-league hockey franchise.

Hockey fans like these deserved a team. This city deserved a team. And the effing Canucks deserved an effing rival. Oh, yeah, he could picture it now. Ethan grinned at the thought of trading trash-talk with some of his Canadian business associates.

Regardless, he forced himself back to the here and now. His team, the Mercer Mets, were playing for the adult league trophy, against the too-many-times champion Bothell Bombers. He'd looked forward to this game all day long—hell, all week long—and had arrived early to take practice shots at the net until he was cross-eyed.

Both teams traded scores in the first two periods until the Bombers took the lead with three minutes remaining in the third. Ethan skated down the ice after a runaway puck only to have Hal Johnson, a dirty player who'd had it out for Ethan all season, slam an elbow into his face. Skidding on his shoulder, Ethan hit the boards head first, sending waves of pain through his neck and back to all parts of his body. Even his dick hurt. Gathering his bruised wits about him and angrier than hell, he shot to his feet, head down, and rammed into Johnson, lifting the asshole off his skates and catapulting him across the ice.

Whistles blew and striped shirts stepped between them before they could do real damage to each other. Ethan attempted to lunge at the asshole but his teammates held him back. Fighting didn't go over very well in this amateur league, but that'd never stopped Johnson before. And Ethan had been known to drop the gloves a time or two when absolutely necessary. He deemed this necessary. Obviously, the referee didn't agree. Within seconds Ethan was cooling his ass in the penalty box.

Fine. Whatever.

He pounded his hockey stick against the boards in a futile effort to spur his team on to winning the trophy.

The Mercer Mets' goalie, a convenience store clerk who spent every spare penny on hockey equipment and fees, pushed up his mask to wipe away the sweat then hunkered down again as Bothell Bombers skated toward his net. Nat, the Mets' best defenseman and a laid-off Boeing machinist, cut off the Bombers' center and took a hack at the puck. Not pretty, but it shot down the ice away from the net where Syd, their top scorer and a city cop, sped after it and a hit slap shot toward the net. It missed by a fraction.

Ethan glanced at the scoreboard. Seconds left. Leaping to his feet, he shouted encouragement, but it was too late. The final buzzer sounded. With a heavy sigh, Ethan skated back onto the ice to shake hands with the opposing team like the good sport he really wasn't. Except for Johnson. Instead, he trash-talked the jerk as he walked by and engaged in a pushing match until their respective teammates pried them apart once more. Since he wasn't going to get any satisfaction, Ethan headed for the locker room, sad to see the season end. It'd been damn fun while it lasted, but there was always next year.

"Ethan." Cyrus, his attorney, stopped him short as he stepped off the ice.

"Did you come to watch me skate like crap and blow the game for the guys, Cy?" Ethan managed a grin despite how pissed he was at himself. Sure it was just a game in an adult league, but he hated losing. Hell, it could've been a pickup game of basketball in the parking lot and he'd treat it like the NBA finals.

Cy was grinning, and Ethan went on red alert. He doubted that grin was because Cyrus enjoyed Ethan's pain—which the bastard usually did.

"What is it?" Ethan asked.

"They're ready, E." Cyrus kept grinning, and Ethan could not for the life of him understand what *they* were ready for.

"Ready?" Ethan halted and squinted at his friend, not making sense of the words. That blow he'd taken to the head earlier must've done more damage than he'd originally thought.

"All our hard work is about to pay off." Cy looked about to pee his pants from excitement.

Ethan went still inside as Cy's words sank into his thick skull. His heart stopped beating. His lungs stopped heaving. Nothing moved. Not an eyelash.

Cy waited patiently, still grinning.

"What did you say?" Ethan pushed dark hair off his forehead and wiped his face with a towel Nat tossed his way.

Cy glanced around, grabbed Ethan by the arm, and led him to a more private area at the end of a long hallway. "The Sleezers want to sell. The league is on board. Everything's in place but with the stipulation the sale be kept absolutely quiet as long as the Giants are in the playoffs." Cyrus, a hockey fan in his own right, hopped from one foot to the other as if he were walking over hot coals. His hips swayed, and he danced to the disco music constantly playing in his head. He wouldn't win *Dancing with the Stars*, but Ethan gave him points for enthusiasm.

"Playoffs?" Ethan said.

"Yeah, the Giants made the playoffs tonight by a thread."

Ethan sat down hard on one of the plastic chairs lining the hallway, looking up at Cyrus. "As late as last week, the Sleezers swore they'd go down with their sinking ship."

"That was before they lost a harassment lawsuit to a few former employees. Now a couple hundred million in their pockets is looking damn good." Cyrus checked his watch. "I have the private jet idling on the tarmac at Boeing Field to get us there before the flakes change their minds. Again."

"Damn. Finally." Ethan could feel the smile spreading across his face. He leapt to his feet and punched his fist in the air. "Yes, yes, yes."

Cyrus grinned back as Ethan started to pace in the hallway, his mind going a million miles a minute as he ran through everything they'd need to do in the next twenty-four hours to tie up the purchase before the Sleezers had a chance to get cold feet.

"Did you call Reynolds?" Ethan asked.

Brad Reynolds had been Ethan's best friend since junior high football. The Reynolds family represented old Seattle money. Even if their fortune might be somewhat diminished of late, they still commanded instant respect and brandished major political clout. That political clout was proving to be more valuable than cash when it came to getting permits approved for a new ice arena. Brad, the middle Reynolds brother, had jumped on board immediately as the family representative, while his two brothers, parents, and a sister came along for the ride as somewhat silent partners. None of them knew a damn thing about hockey, but they loved sports and were more than willing to learn.

"Yeah, Brad's on his way. He'll meet us at Boeing Field."

Ethan checked his watch. Six-thirty on a Saturday. It was going to be a long but profitable night. "Crap. Let me shower, and I'll be out in fifteen."

Ethan made it out in nine minutes. The only reason he wasn't quicker was because of the required commiserating with his teammates over the abrupt end of their season.

Several hours later, Ethan and Brad signed on the dotted line as majority shareholders and main representatives of the Puget Sound Hockey Alliance.

Seattle had a professional hockey team.

Only no one could know it.

Not yet.

* * * *

For the first thirty years of his life, Ethan concentrated on building his family's already massive fortune, but making money had lost its luster. The thrill had gone. With his family's blessing, he'd turned to a different pursuit. The Parkers were good citizens, and good citizens gave back to their community. Ethan's gift to Seattle manifested itself in the form of a state-of-the-art hockey arena. Of course, now he needed a team to play in it.

He had pursued that goal with a single-minded purpose, amassing a who's-who of Seattle businessmen, along with the Reynolds family, to be part of his merry band of marauders bent on stealing a struggling hockey franchise from another city and resurrecting it in Seattle. He'd worked zealously in the background, never showing his face, never tipping his hand. He was the man behind the mirror—the Emerald City's hockey wizard.

He would've preferred an expansion team, but he was an impatient man, and impatient men took advantage of their opportunities.

After the signing of the sales papers, Ethan, Cyrus, and Brad dragged their asses to an all-night diner. As usual, the Sleezers had jacked them around, hemming and hawing and spouting all this bullshit about hockey being in their blood and how difficult this was for the family to abandon their legacy. Ethan wanted to throw up. Over the past several years, the brothers systematically raided the team coffers to finance their own pleasures and had shown zero interest in the team itself. Finally, Ethan and Cyrus played hardball with the jerks, calling their bluff, and going so far as to walk out of the room. They didn't get far before the Sleezers' attorney ran after them. Things proceeded quickly after that, and the sales agreements were signed, and the deed was done.

Ethan leaned forward in the booth with his hands wrapped around a cup of coffee. Brad and Cyrus sat opposite him, also deep in thought. Most people took Brad at face value, considering him a shallow playboy. Ethan knew better. Behind Brad's easy smile and smooth-talking lurked a guy with as much determination as Ethan to see this thing through and create a winning tradition of hockey in Seattle. Ethan expected nothing less of his partner in crime.

"When are we flying back?" Brad finally turned his head away from his study of a beach volleyball game playing on the one TV in the diner.

"I'm not. I'm staying on. This is a prime opportunity to study every aspect of the team during the season, and I'm taking advantage of it."

"But the league and the Sleezers put a gag order on your pending purchase and the team's subsequent move. If anyone leaks information about the offer before the final game of the season, the deal is off, especially since we're moving the team," Cyrus reminded him with one of those looks Ethan knew so well.

"I know. I was there, too. Remember? But I have options. It's no secret the team is in financial straits and destined to be sold."

Brad nodded and smiled. "I can see your devious mind spinning."

"I'm taking a page out that TV show where the boss goes undercover."

"Seriously? Are you going to wear a wig and a mustache, too?" Cyrus snorted with laughter, finding this way too amusing.

Ethan sighed. Sometimes, he swore these two didn't have a serious bone in their bodies. "I'll be using a different last name. I'm not recognizable because I've avoided the limelight. I'll get an insider's view of the team from top to bottom, from the first line to the fourth line, from the GM to the administrative assistant. I'll evaluate who'll make the move to Seattle and who needs to go."

"How are you going undercover?" Brad asked.

"As a representative for a potential buyer to determine the team's worth and its investment potential."

Cyrus nodded. "Clever. People will be more likely to give you the honest scoop if they believe you can't fire them, but they'll be pissed as hell when they find out you've duped them."

Ethan shrugged, no stranger to pissing people off. Not that he made a habit of it, but his drive and ambition often did that job for him. "This isn't a popularity contest. This is about winning."

And that, to Ethan, was the bottom line.

* * * *

Lauren Schneider rolled over in bed and frowned at the cell laying on the nightstand, its face illuminated by an incoming call.

Who the hell called a person at six-thirty AM on a Sunday unless it was an emergency?

Usually she was already awake at this hour, ready to attack the day, but the Gainesville Giants hockey team had advanced to the playoffs for the first time in years with their win over Ottawa last night. Of course, it helped that the league had increased the number of playoff teams recently, which opened up wildcard slots not available in the past. After the win, she'd attended the team party to celebrate. Lauren usually didn't participate in such parties, but she made an exception last night, and in the process imbibed a little too much.

Only one troubling fact had marred an otherwise perfect evening. The game hadn't sold out. In fact, it came well short of it. The guys deserved better, but the Sleezer brothers were too busy spending the team proceeds to be bothered with promoting the team. Plus, who wanted to sit in a hockey arena when it was eighty degrees outside? Not that she bought that excuse. Other warm-weather teams didn't have a problem drawing a crowd, but the Sleezers had produced such a lousy product for long enough that fans had deserted the team in droves. Disappointed, they'd gravitated to other sports teams in the area, except for a handful of diehards the team fondly called the faithful fifty, even though their numbers were greater than fifty. It just didn't look like that on most days.

Lauren glanced at the phone and frowned. It was her boss, Terry Allen, the director of player personnel. A call from him this early in the morning probably meant one thing—one of the guys had gotten in trouble and needed to be bailed out of jail or worse. She'd work her spin magic with the marketing staff while Terry took care of the player.

As assistant director of player personnel for an organization in financial trouble, Lauren's role had morphed into something of a Girl Friday, as the Sleezers continued to cut staff to make payroll and maintain their extravagant lifestyle. It hadn't always been like this, but after the patriarch of the family died six years ago, things had gone downhill faster than a runaway train.

"This better be good, Allen." She worked hard to maintain her kick-ass female rep, and she didn't let down, even with the man who signed her paychecks.

"Get to HQ, and you needed to be here about fifteen minutes

ago."

"What's going on?"

"Get your ass down here." He hung up the phone. In itself that wasn't unusual. Terry wasn't known for his touchy-feely conversations, so it probably meant nothing.

Lauren showered, dressed, and was in her car speeding to the arena, where the team had its headquarters, in record time. Because her life was all about the team, she lived five minutes away, fifteen minutes if she walked, but she didn't have time for walking today.

Scenarios raced through Lauren's mind. *The Sleezers declared bankruptcy—finally? Or team captain Cooper Black was in jail? Cedric got caught in a compromising position with a woman or several women? Nah, that wouldn't be news. Maybe all those sales rumors finally came to fruition? The league had tired of bailing out the Sleezers? Or—or what?*

Lauren hurried into the building, relatively empty except for janitorial staff cleaning up from the party last night.

She nodded to the gray-haired guy sitting behind the security desk. "Hey, Herm, how goes it?"

"Big stuff going down here last night, missy. Lots of important men in and out, including the commissioner."

"The commissioner was here?" Oh, God, this *was* big. Way big. Scary big. "Any idea why?"

Herm frowned and pulled his lips in a tight line which said all she was getting out of him would be name and rank, and forget about the serial number. "You'd best go upstairs and find out for yourself."

She headed for the stairs, glancing over her shoulder at Herm. He tried to smile but failed. Herm always found something to smile about, no matter what. Not so today.

The place was quiet as she walked down the long hallway of the empty offices of the team, but she heard laughter coming from the conference room—even what she swore was the popping of a champagne cork. Lauren stuck her head around the partially open door. Terry motioned her inside. She hesitated when she saw the general manager and coach in the office along with several other staff members, all with grins on their faces, which is what one would expect from a team advancing to the playoffs for the first time in a decade. So what was the problem?

"Who's in jail?" Lauren quipped.

"No one." Ike McGrady, the GM, shook his head, and almost managed a smile. Ike was like an uncle to her. He'd played in the league with her father. While he'd been an incredible forward, his management skills left a lot to be desired, but Lauren never spoke up against him, despite the grumblings among the staff. Ike moved at a snail's pace when it came to decisions. His inability to jump on a deal quickly had lost them a good many players over the years.

"Did the Sleezers lose their minds and give all of us big raises?" Lauren asked.

"Nope, not even close," Ike grouched, but Ike liked to grouch. He could win the Mega Millions and be pissed about it.

"Then did I miss a memo or something?"

Terry nodded. "Pretty much. We all did."

"I don't understand." Lauren tucked a stray strand of light brown hair behind one ear.

"Now that we're all here, let's get started." Everyone looked to Ike in his rumpled shirt, tie askew. His rubbed his bloodshot eyes but still managed a tired, yet happy, smile. "The league is forcing the Sleezers to sell, and we have a potential buyer."

Obviously this was news to everyone except Terry, Ike, and Coach Ferrar.

"Seriously? Who?" They lived through these rumors every couple months; never before had it justified an early Sunday meeting. The Sleezer brothers, not-so-fondly known around the team headquarters as the Sleazes, had gone back and forth about selling the team while they bled it dry in order to finance their yacht, mansions, parties, and women. Upstanding citizens, the Sleazes. It was no secret the league wanted them banned from hockey's exclusive club of owners.

"We don't know other than they have deep pockets. Very deep."

"This team deserves deep pockets and decent owners who'll build on what we've done." Lauren could tell by Ike's lack of a frown that he agreed. Losing the Sleezers was a damn good thing.

"Why are we meeting at O-dark-thirty? Couldn't this wait until Monday?" Kaley, the head coach's executive assistant and Lauren's best friend, blinked her eyes and yawned. Last Lauren had seen of her, she'd been dancing on a table with one of the rookies, wearing an ice bucket on her head, and doing tequila shots.

"It can't wait. The league is putting on the pressure." Ike

appeared to be nursing a hangover himself.

"What kind of pressure?" Lauren honestly didn't understand why they were here early Sunday morning after the team had won their biggest game in years.

"Money talks and the league listens." Ike rubbed his eyes, looking worse than Lauren felt. "The prospective buyers are sending a couple representatives to vet the team, and the league wants us to play nice and be on our best behavior."

"Who are these guys?" Terry asked the question that was on the tip of everyone's tongue.

"No one knows." Ike grimaced. He obviously hated not knowing what he was getting into and with whom.

"Someone does," Lauren pointed out the obvious. "Or they wouldn't have ordered us to kiss their asses."

"They'll be here on Monday and underfoot at every game from this point forward."

"As in tomorrow?" Lauren was still in shock, trying to process what these changes meant to the team, the staff, and her. "This is a good thing, right?"

"Getting rid of the Sleezers can only be a good thing," Terry answered.

A smattering of applause erupted around the room. No one would dispute that fact.

"They aren't planning on moving the team, are they?" Lauren asked.

Ike smiled, but Lauren caught the concern that flashed in his eyes. "Ah, Lauren, ever the skeptic. To my knowledge, there are no plans to move the team."

Lauren couldn't help being skeptical. Her life consisted of a long line of promises made and never kept, starting with her beloved father who put hockey over family until her mother divorced him and embraced being a bitter, vindictive woman. Then Lauren repeated her mother's mistake by marrying a hockey player herself, and that sure as hell hadn't ended well.

"We meet with these guys first thing Monday morning. In the meantime, we need to be ready for any questions they ask us. The Sleezers must go, and it's up to us to make sure these guys don't leave Florida without a recommendation to their bosses to buy the team. I expect every one of you to play nice with them and give them the information they request, of course, while putting the organization in the most positive light possible."

Lauren nodded. Getting rid of the Sleezers seemed almost too good to be true.

Which was exactly why it made her nervous.

Chapter 2—Playing His Game

Ethan never went into a situation unprepared, especially a potentially volatile one.

Before he walked into the building on Monday, he knew everything about every staff person down to the security guy and the janitor.

He stood at the head of the table in a packed conference room consisting of Giants' management and coaches. Making eye contact with each and every person there, he mentally checked off their names based on pictures and video he'd studied. They stared back at him with hopeful expressions on their faces, as if he was their savior not their dismantler. Ethan felt a twinge of guilt, even remorse, over what he was about to do, but he tamped it down. There was no room for emotions in business dealings, and he'd never allowed them to color his decisions in the past. They wouldn't now.

None of the research done by his Seattle staff had prepared him for Lauren Schneider—the woman he'd secretly handpicked to be his team liaison. Lauren was smart, ambitious, and as a woman in a man's world was bent on proving herself in this male-dominated sport. Best of all, she had a brilliant hockey mind. All perfect qualities for the type of person he needed to give him an insider's knowledge.

She didn't look a thing like her father, but she did have his attitude, and Ethan liked attitude—to a point. Lauren wore a functional pair of shoes and a conservative business suit with a knee-length skirt. No stilettos for this woman. Her brown hair was confined to a tight bun at the back of her head.

Actually, she'd be quite pretty if she played up her assets instead of downplaying them. He'd like to see her cinnamon brown hair falling in soft waves about her face. God, she had the most kissable pink lips and expressive hazel eyes. Ethan had a secret affinity for old movies. She reminded him of Lauren Bacall even down to the exotic shape of her eyes and her cute nose, and he had no business thinking about her physical attributes or comparing her to a forties film siren.

Even so, the minimal makeup and business suit did nothing to hide the attractive woman sitting before him, arms crossed over a nice pair and a scowl on her pretty face. He almost laughed, but laughing at her bad-ass façade wouldn't exactly earn points with her, and he needed to win her over to his side.

He'd have to relax her a little so she'd fit in in Seattle—if she went to Seattle with the team. A true Pacific Northwesterner dressed in jeans and sweatshirts, even wearing good jeans to nice restaurants. Northwest casual they called it. Ethan liked casual. With Lauren's buttoned-up style, he wasn't sure if he liked her—not yet, but he didn't give a shit. As long as she furnished him with the required information, he'd be fine with that.

She watched him with more wariness than the others, as if she wasn't as easily won over. He was fine with that, too. Liking him wasn't a job requirement.

Brad didn't take a seat but stood against the wall at the opposite end of the room, getting a view of the group Ethan didn't have. His partner appeared to be paying attention and watching with an unusual intensity. Sometimes Brad surprised him. The work he'd done to secure the arena and this team went above and beyond with an enthusiasm Brad rarely displayed for activities outside of partying and women.

Ethan pulled his attention back to the hopeful faces gazing up at him from around the room.

Ike, the GM, cleared his throat, garnering the attention of everyone in the room. "I apologize for calling all of you in so early on a Monday morning. As you know, the league has long been interested in seeking new ownership for this franchise. As a result, they've hired an independent consultant to assess the value of this team and report back to the interested parties. Ethan Williams will be working with us, as will his partner Brad Reese. Please give them your utmost cooperation." Ike indicated Ethan and took a seat, giving Ethan the floor.

"Thank you all for coming." Ethan paused, swept his gaze around the room, and did a quick assessment to determine the receptiveness of the staff and coaches. Lauren's direct stare was more of a challenge than anything, seeming to say, prove to me you can help this team.

A smile tugged at the corner of his mouth because of her intensity, as if this was the most important thing on earth—and to her it obviously was. He'd done his research, and she appeared to be the type of employee he wanted to retain. Not a "yes" person or a member of the good ol' boys, but an employee who'd give him the straight scoop whether he liked what she had to say or not.

He'd made the right choice when it came to her showing him around.

"I'll make this short, as you have playoffs to concentrate on. Congratulations on a job well done in the midst of a difficult situation."

A small smattering of applause sounded around the room. He'd earned a few points with that remark.

He turned his attention back to Lauren. Despite her librarian appearance, she was easy on the eyes. Let his sister get a hold of her, and Rebecca would turn her into a stunner. Realizing he was gawking, Ethan cleared his throat. "I'm going to need a staff person to take me under their wing and show me the ropes. It was suggested that Lauren be my guide."

He nodded at Lauren. She pursed her lips, and her eyes narrowed with suspicion.

Several of the men murmured their agreement, probably glad they didn't have to babysit him.

Ethan spoke briefly about not much of anything in an attempt to put them at ease, maybe mislead them a bit regarding his hockey knowledge without actually lying. After all, his mere presence here was a big enough lie.

As everyone filed out, he signaled for Lauren to stay. She approached him with that same wariness, yet he must have won her over slightly because he also noted hopefulness in her expression. He forced his gaze to remain above her neck, but he wouldn't be a man if he hadn't briefly noticed her curvy body and shapely legs. She was probably a good seven to eight inches shorter than his six-foot-two, yet she stood straight and proud with as much presence as any man.

"Mr. Williams," she nodded. "Where would you like to start?" For a moment, he wondered who she was addressing until he mentally kicked himself. He and Brad had chosen fake last names, and he'd almost messed it up within a few minutes of meeting the staff. Damn, he'd never been good with deception. He preferred the straight-forward approach, but this situation didn't allow him that luxury.

"Lauren, call me Ethan." He shot her one of his woman-melting smiles, but she froze instead. "I'm a huge fan of your father's. I'll never forget his winning goal in the Gold Medal game against Canada."

Lauren nodded tersely, as if no amount of flattery would get him anywhere with her. Fine, he'd keep it strictly business and dispense with the niceties.

"Let's get down to business, shall we? I understand you're quite the evaluator of hockey talent."

"I hold my own. I was raised in a hockey rink." Lauren met his gaze. For the first time in their brief conversation, she seemed caught off balance, as if his words of praise were unexpected and uncommon. Not surprising for a woman fighting to make it in a man's world.

He knew she was the youngest of three and the only girl. Her parents were divorced, and she'd traded time between her mother's home in Florida and her father in New York. She'd graduated with a bachelor's in sports management from the University of Michigan. She had the credentials and the bloodlines to be a great asset to a hockey team, but she'd been passed over time and again because of her lack of a penis. As a favor to her father, the Giants hired her years ago as an administrative assistant, and she'd scratched and clawed her way up. She was a fighter, this one, just like her father and brothers. And her name sat at the top of his initial keeper list.

"I'm a hands-on guy. I'm going to be in everyone's back pocket for the next month or two or at least until the team's season ends—hopefully with the Cup."

"Wonderful." She stared at him as if trying to figure out what made him tick, most likely assessing him for weaknesses she might need to exploit. "You're not a hockey guy, are you?"

Ethan bristled, fully aware he wasn't part of the good ol' boys' hockey club. "What makes you think that?"

"Because I know everyone in this league and I don't know you."

Ethan opened his mouth to defend himself then thought better of it. If she believed he didn't have hockey knowledge, she could let valuable information slip, information she might not normally give in order to protect the people she worked with and the team she supported.

No one knew he played adult hockey with a fervor that matched an NHL player's. No one needed to know he'd lived and breathed hockey for years, having been initiated into the sport by a Canadian bachelor uncle who lived in Vancouver.

"I don't consider that relevant. I'm evaluating this team from a business and an investment point of view. You're here to help me get to know the players, stuff I won't learn from game tape or reading online articles. I assure you, what I lack in hockey knowledge I'll make up for with sheer dogged determination."

She stared at him with an unreadable expression and made no comment.

"I need to meet with the coaching staff. When I return, we'll go over each player's strengths and weaknesses. A high level but accurate assessment. I'm a big picture person. For example, where do these guys fit in the organization? Who's an asset? Who's a determent?"

"I know how to do my job," she said with a tight-lipped frown.

He left her office, feeling a bit like an ass, yet aware this situation could get out of control pretty fast if he didn't squelch the first sign of concern from the team or the staff.

Still, her hazel eyes staring at him with suspicion didn't make what he had to do any easier. Not to mention his instant attraction to her, which didn't happen often to him. The few times it had proved disastrous. He would not endanger his purchase of this team by having a dalliance with an employee, especially an employee he might want to keep.

Very few of these people would be going to Seattle with him. He valued loyalty above all else, and he needed to figure out who was one-hundred-percent loyal to the team itself, and not to the good ol' boys club which had been controlling this team for close to two decades.

* * * *

Lauren had stepped over the line. She'd talked back to the man, and his blue eyes had blazed, not with anger as much as a challenge, one she didn't wholly understand.

The next several weeks would be pure, absolute torture. Not only was Ethan an enigma, but he was attractive as hell. With that same sixth sense which made her a wizard at evaluating hockey talent, she sensed there was more to Ethan than he'd revealed. He was hiding something, and that unknown made her uncomfortable and intrigued at the same time, not to mention she was hot for him. She'd be a liar to deny it. He looked more like a male model than a consultant with his jet black hair and sky blue eyes. Those broad shoulders filled out his suit perfectly, and she could only imagine what his body looked like underneath. The man himself was drop-dead gorgeous, just the type Lauren had a weakness for and that made him doubly dangerous.

As she pondered this bewildering mess in which she'd found herself immersed, Kaley peeked around the door. "What did you say to him?"

"Probably too much. I don't trust him."

Kaley glanced over her shoulder and then back. "You don't trust most men in this business."

Lauren shrugged. Kaley spoke the truth.

"Did you see the hot guy with him?"

Lauren thought Ethan was pretty damn hot for a businessman. "Uh, I hadn't noticed."

Kaley narrowed her eyes and studied Lauren. "Don't you dare go crushing on Ethan Williams."

"Look at you. Warning me while you're drooling over his associate."

"I am not, even if he is sexy as hell, and I have an orgasm looking at him. But orgasmically sexy doesn't mean anything. It's all look and no touch. I don't date rich pricks with an ego bigger than Cedric's." Cedric was their charismatic forward, who played as hard off the ice as he did on it.

"So you just date poor pricks or what?"

"I do have a soft spot for them." Kaley shrugged one shoulder and studied her fingernails.

"You have a soft spot for good-looking men in general, forget about their personalities."

Kaley was a serial dater, and Lauren lived vicariously through her since dating didn't seem to be her forte, and her taste in men left a lot to be desired. Her life revolved around hockey and unless the man was on skates, had a wicked slapshot, or an even more wicked right hook, she wasn't interested. Of course, she didn't date hockey players, at least not anymore. She'd taken a few for a spin around the rink in her college days and decided they made better friends than lovers, except for the one she'd married. That biggest mistake of her life drove home the no dating of hockey players creed, which she'd amended to any man involved in hockey just to play it safe.

Kaley wagged a finger at her. "Just remember, play nice. The league has been trying to land a buyer forever that would keep the team in Florida. So let's hope this guy gives a favorable report to his bosses, or we'll be sold to that Seattle group who've been circling like sharks smelling blood. Next thing you know, we'll be sipping lattes on the waterfront while watching ferry boats putter around."

"In the pouring rain."

"Well, there is that," Kaley acknowledged with a toss of her dark hair.

"How do we know this guy isn't working for the Seattle group?" Lauren frowned as she put to words fears she'd been harboring since yesterday.

For a moment a cloud passed over Kaley's face, then she smiled, slipping back into her create-my-own-reality mode. "Because Ike said he didn't think the team was moving."

Just thinking of Seattle shot dread through Lauren. She didn't have a thing against Seattle, but she was an East Coast girl through and through. Moss and mold made her sneeze. Huge trees and mountains gave her claustrophobia. And the geeks Seattle was famous for didn't buy hockey tickets, did they?

A tall man with dark blond hair and dancing blue eyes poked his head in the doorway. "Hey, I'm looking for Ethan." He turned a panty-dropping smile on Lauren, but it lingered on Kaley. As usual, most men couldn't get past her long black hair, curvy body, and dark, mysterious eyes. "Hey, hi, again."

Kaley literally purred as she stepped next to the guy and wrapped her fingers around his arm. "Hi, yourself. Brad, you know Lauren Schneider, our assistant director of player personnel?"

Brad smiled at her. "So you're the poor girl who gets to babysit *the man*. Good luck. He's a handful."

"I'm sure I can handle him just fine."

Kaley, in full flirt mode, batted thick eyelashes at Brad. "Let's see if we can find Ethan. Lauren has work to do."

Brad laughed, a full-throated laugh. "As long as she's the one doing the work, and it isn't us." He came across as the type of guy a girl couldn't help but like—gregarious, fun, and not a mean bone in his body.

Together Brad and Kaley strolled down the hall in the opposite direction of where Ethan happened to be meeting with the coaches.

Lauren shook her head. Leave it to Kaley to hustle the hot guy. But anything that helped their cause was more than worth it, as long as it wasn't Lauren doing the hustling.

With a sigh she went back to work on her statistics and spreadsheets, making notes here and there and jotting down items for Ethan's attention, items which painted the current team and staff in a positive light.

Anything for the good of the team.

Chapter 3—Breakaway

On Wednesday, Ethan took his seat on the glass near the players' bench for the first round of the playoff series between the Giants and Montreal. The entire team and selected staff had flown into Montreal by private jet the night before. Ethan insisted on being on that jet, observing and forming impressions, just like he insisted on sitting on the glass tonight. He needed to be on top of the action for the first playoff game to assess how the team interacted with each other and the coaching staff, to study their weaknesses and strengths, and evaluate each line. He'd already watched endless film from an overhead view, but being down on the glass gave him a completely different perspective, up close and personal, of how the team worked together on the ice.

Ethan opened up his iPad and tapped some notes about the players as they warmed up. The first line was as good as any in pro hockey. Cooper Black was the undisputed leader of the team, fast and aggressive, their top scorer and near the top in assists, too. Next to him at right wing skated Cedric Pedersen, a strong Swede who could power a puck into the net. At left wing, a young guy, Drew Delacorte, was still raw but had the talent. Martin "Brick" Bricker, in his second year, played goalie with enthusiasm and heart, though his inexperience would come through at the worst of times. On defense, Matt LeRue skated his ass off, quick, strong, and not afraid to mix it up when needed. The guy handled the puck like a baby in his arms. Jason "Wildman" Wilder was the other half of the defensive combo and fought for possession like a crazed man.

The guys worked well together, but Ethan didn't believe they were good enough to get past the first round, considering the second and third lines were an unremarkable average. The team needed an overhaul, and he needed a coach and GM with the guts to do it. But he wasn't here to prove or disprove his initial impressions, and he kept an open mind. There might be players with untapped talent who'd shine when paired up with the right line to capitalize on their strengths.

Ethan glanced up as Lauren slid into the seat next to him. She nodded, took stock of his iPad, and raised one eyebrow, a smile tugging at one corner of her mouth. She held a similar device along with a tablet of yellow-lined paper. Obviously embracing the old and the new.

He liked that.

He also liked how good she smelled, which somewhat threw him for a loop. So did that little uptick in his heart rate and a slight shortness of breath, all signs he was attracted to a woman. A bad idea considering how horribly his only dalliance with a woman on his payroll had ended. Not that Lauren was technically on his payroll. Yet.

Regardless, he couldn't help but notice her curvy body in her standard-issue suit, nice ass, and even nicer rack, even though she dressed to disguise her figure. Tonight not so much. This suit fit a little tighter than the others he'd seen, not to mention a slightly shorter skirt. He liked that shorter skirt, but she needed to lose the damn bun. He could help with that. Then again, he'd better abandon that line of thinking.

Their eyes met and that little uptick kicked up a notch or two—ah, hell, maybe three. Lauren looked away quickly, almost as if flustered, which left him feeling a little smug that she felt the chemistry, too.

Lauren woke up her tablet and started reading through stuff. Ethan leaned over to get a better look. She handed it to him. He was impressed. This team seemed a little behind the times, but these detailed stats were usually employed by the more progressive teams. Endless detailed stats, from the first drop of the puck to the final buzzer. It was all there.

"I'm impressed. You keep advanced analytics."

Lauren's face colored in the most attractive shade of dark pink. "Yes, but so far I haven't convinced the coaching staff as to their usefulness."

"A little old school, are they?" He asked conversationally.

She opened her mouth, appeared to think better of whatever she was about to say, and snapped it shut. "They'll come around."

Ethan nodded, fully aware he needed to earn her trust before she'd reveal any telling details about the staff, especially the coaches. Players would be another thing. After all, this was business, and she was good at her job, so she had to have opinions on where they were lacking.

"What do you think of the first line? They seem strong. Second line seems solid, but I'm not sold on that third and fourth line."

Lauren hesitated then launched into a detailed analysis of each player's strengths and weaknesses from the first line to the fourth line that would have done her father proud. It sure as hell impressed Ethan. She pointed out things he hadn't picked up on, while her advanced statistics revealed the true workhorses on the team, guys who carried the team yet might not show up in the usual statistics because they may not have scored the goal, but their actions led up to it.

Ethan sat back and let her talk. Details didn't usually excite him, but the challenge of putting all the pieces together into a winning organization compelled him to listen to her, not to mention he loved the sound of her voice and the way her eyes turned a deep green when she was passionate about something. He almost groaned as he imagined how green they'd be in the midst of an orgasm.

Shit.

The puck dropped and the game started. Lauren stopped mid-sentence and focused on the men driving up and down the ice. Ethan rubbed the back of his neck, aroused by how intently she watched the game. Just like him when he wasn't watching her. Turning his attention to the ice, he leaned forward and gripped the armrests, his body following the movements of certain players as if he were on the ice with them. Even as involved as he was in watching his team play, he never forgot the woman sitting next to him.

Lauren offered occasional tidbits of information on particular players. He'd never met a female with such an extensive knowledge of hockey. Even better, she had a great eye for talent, which was equally impressive. If there'd ever been any doubt, he knew without reservation he wanted her in Seattle, and he'd do what it took to keep her.

If only he could explain who and what he was doing so his deception wouldn't come between them when the sale was announced. But he couldn't. The league had effectively shut that door and locked it. The gag order said it all. Leakage of information on this purchase agreement meant no team. And he wanted this team in the worst way.

But there was something else he wanted which shocked the hell out of him. He wanted *Lauren* in the worst way. He'd never expected to be attracted to her. Maybe it was her subtle sexuality, her complete openness, and lack of pretenses. She was who she was, and if you didn't like it, too bad for you.

Most of the women he knew played games. Not this woman.

Ethan shook his head, trying to clear it. He was here for one reason and one reason only—the culmination of his dream to bring hockey to Seattle.

He wanted Lauren on his team, but he could not want her in his bed, for a myriad of reasons.

Tell that to his dick because it had other ideas.

Tough luck, it was staying on the bench.

* * * *

Lauren followed Ethan to the arena concourse. The Giants lost a heartbreaking game, and thinking about it made Lauren sick to her stomach.

Right now she should be thinking life didn't get better than this. Despite their first loss, they were still in it, skating in their first playoff series in years, and next to her stood a man who might well be the team's savior, and he was an incredibly attractive man.

His eyes lit up with unbridled enthusiasm every time they discussed the team and its potential, almost as if he had a personal stake in the Giants, rather than being a hired consultant. She loved the interest he showed in all aspects of the team. Hopefully, his employers shared his enthusiasm.

Yet, his level of enthusiasm and involvement didn't quite fit. Her niggling suspicions that things weren't as they seemed prevented Lauren's complete trust in the man, not that she trusted easily. She'd been burned too many times from family members to friends to lovers to one cheating husband. She'd trusted Max. All the while, he'd been entertaining puck bunnies in every city during his road trips. It made a girl cautious as to whom she granted that precious trust.

Ethan would need to earn her trust by his actions, not his words. Words were cheap and easy to fake. For now, she'd enjoy looking at Ethan, because that was purely a joy, and feeding him positive tidbits about the team and staff.

"I want to see how the coach and team handle the loss," Ethan said, grim determination etched on his handsome face.

"The coach doesn't like anyone in the locker room directly after the game." Lauren hurried after him as he purposely strode into the arena concourse.

Ethan gave her one of those looks which clearly said he didn't give a shit what the coach did or didn't like, but he'd damn well do as he pleased. Turning, he showed security his badge and headed down the tunnel with Lauren on his heels.

"Ethan, this isn't a good idea." The infuriating man kept walking, which really pissed her off. He barged into the locker room with her hot on his heels then stopped so abruptly that she bumped into his backside.

The players sat around the locker room on benches, heads hanging, frowns on their faces, and in various states of undress. Lauren had seen the men many times before in this situation, but this was sacred ground, and Ethan did not belong in here.

Coach Ferrar, fondly known as Coach Fur by staff and team alike, stopped mid-sentence and glared at the unwelcome intruders. While Coach wanted the Sleezers out of team ownership, he, like Lauren, didn't exactly trust Ethan, and even worse, he hated change. As Lauren saw it, the coach figured the devil he knew—the Sleezers—was better than the devil he didn't, in the form of Ethan and his anonymous employers.

At the coach's silence, every player glanced up, their gazes shifting from Coach to Ethan and back to Coach. They held their collective breaths, as if sensing a good fight in the making, and Lauren bet their money was on Coach. She wasn't so sure.

She glanced at Ethan, who didn't seem the least bit affected by the coach's laser sharp gaze. "Just pretend I'm not here."

"It'd be better if you weren't," Coach Fur growled.

Ethan didn't move. Instead he smiled as if Coach couldn't possibly be referring to him.

"Look, I know we've been ordered to cater to you, and God knows we want the Sleezers out of ownership, but that doesn't mean you can walk in here like you own the place. This is private business between the team and coaches."

A muscle ticked in Ethan's strong jaw, but his calm voice echoed through the silent room. "I'm examining all aspects of this team for the prospective owners, including the locker room atmosphere."

The team captain, Cooper Black, muttered something to his

buddy, Cedric.

"What was that, Black? You got something to say, say it so I can hear it," Ethan challenged him.

Coop's eyes narrowed, and he met Ethan's direct gaze with a pointed one of his own. "I said since when do owners—prospective or otherwise—give a shit about what goes on in the locker room as long as we win on the ice?"

"This group does. They're very hands-on."

"Great, just what we need. Owners who think they can tell me how to coach." Coach slapped his clipboard against his thigh, obviously beyond annoyed. Several of the guys nodded their heads in agreement.

"And me how to play," Cooper didn't seem impressed with Ethan or his billionaire employers.

"I've interrupted enough. I'll fade into the background. Continue as if I'm not here." Ethan wasn't the least bit moved by their words, or put off. He just shrugged and took a seat as if he was one of the guys. Lauren wrung her hands and tried to think of a way to get him out of there. No one came into the locker room directly after the game. No one. Coach would have her head for letting Ethan in. Not that she could have stopped him.

Ethan sat back as if he were in a movie theatre and the show was about to begin. Lauren wanted to throttle the man with her bare hands.

Realizing their unwelcome guest wasn't leaving, the coach turned to his team. "It's only game one. We know a lot more about our opponents than we did yesterday. We'll get them tomorrow. That's it, guys. Meet back here in the morning, usual time."

Lauren suspected he purposely didn't say what time to keep Ethan out of the loop. The team stood, going back to their post-game routines. Ethan met Lauren's gaze and raised a decidedly amused eyebrow.

"Don't you think we should leave now?" she asked.

Ethan sighed and stood. He held the door open for her, and she gladly exited from the locker room. As soon as they were in the hallway, she turned on him. "What did you think you were doing?"

"I told you. I'm evaluating the team and its operations." His calm voice infuriated her even more, and she did have a bit of her father's temper.

31

"And that includes invading the sacred sanctuary of the coach's post-game speech?"

"It especially means that. I wanted to see how coaches and players handled the loss. How a team handles losing is more important than how they handle winning. Do they mope, do they get fired up, do they hang their heads in defeat, or do they immediately look to the next game and what they can do better?"

"They handled the loss fine, but they didn't handle you fine."

"They'll get used to me." Ethan stared over her head, focusing on the GM and other staff members standing in the hallway with a few sports reporters.

"They don't need to. You're a temporary fixture around here."

His head snapped back around to her. Something flashed briefly across his face. Had it been guilt? Had she read too much into it? Could someone as bold and self-centered as Ethan even feel guilt? And if he did, what did he have to feel guilty about? Lauren's stomach tightened with dread, dread of the unknown.

The man had secrets, and she didn't know if he was the team's savior or the team's destroyer. "Look, I know you're not a hockey guy—"

"Which you remind me of every chance you get."

"Because you're an arrogant, stubborn—" Lauren stopped and shoved her knuckles in her mouth. She wanted—needed—to keep this job. A job this high up in a pro organization was damn near impossible for a man to get, let alone a woman, and she was sure as hell doing a bang-up job of screwing it up.

"Go on, I'm a big boy. I can take it." Ethan leaned back against the concrete block wall of the hallway. He crossed his arms over his chest.

Lauren stared at her feet, closed her eyes for a moment, then raised her head. "That was out of line. I shouldn't have said that."

He shrugged one shoulder, regarding her with half-lidded eyes. "Sure you should have. Are you afraid you'll be fired for voicing your opinion and sticking up for your team?" He straightened and leaned in close to her, his face near hers, his pure male scent invading her senses and destroying her ability to think clearly.

"Something like that." Lauren nodded, backing a few feet away from him because his male presence was every bit as powerful as that of any of the professional athletes she worked with on a daily basis. Actually, it was more dangerous because she wasn't attracted to any of them. Not like this. She hadn't felt this magnetic pull since Max.

Instead of following her, he adopted a casual pose, crossing one ankle over the other and leaning an elbow on a nearby cabinet. "Lauren, I'll never hold honesty against you. I value that above all else and so do the people in the ownership group."

Lauren studied him, unable to assess the level of bullshit he might be feeding her, if it was bullshit at all. "I don't know you."

"You will. We'll be spending every waking hour together. You'll learn to trust me. I only want what's best for this team and the ownership group. Remember that. Always." He was trying to tell her something, but Lauren didn't completely buy what he was selling.

He hadn't earned her trust or her allegiance. He wasn't being totally straight with her, and she knew it. Only fools put their trust in a man who didn't speak the truth, but only a portion of it. "Fine, if you mean what you say, you'll listen to me next time and stay out of the locker room."

Ethan opened his mouth to argue then snapped it shut, as if he'd decided to concede that point to her. He chuckled and grinned, a completely disarming grin which left her wondering who the real Ethan was, the hard-nosed, hard-charging businessman or the handsome charmer. She'd rather deal with the businessman because she was too vulnerable to the charmer. "I'll defer to your better judgment next time."

"Thank you." Lauren fought hard to keep the smugness out of her voice. Her daddy had taught her never to be a cocky winner. More often than not, that type of behavior would come back to bite her.

"You're welcome. Let's get some coffee. I'd like to discuss the game."

Several minutes later they sat in a sports bar near the hotel, sipping coffee and comparing notes. Ethan didn't say much, but he certainly listened to every word she said, making notes on his iPad, as he asked insightful questions about every player on the team. Lauren kept her comments positive and criticisms to a minimum.

Finally she sat back and wrapped her hands around her second mug of strong, black coffee. "Tell me what *you* think."

"I'm not a hockey guy, remember?" One corner of his mouth

kicked up in a decidedly sexy half smile.

"You're into sports, correct?"

He nodded. "I played some football and baseball in my day."

She looked him up and down, pondering what position he might have played. Being tall but lean and definitely preferring to be in charge, she guessed immediately. "Quarterback?"

"Which of my sterling qualities gave that away?" He sat back, enjoying himself, and signaled the waitress for a beer, as if to indicate the business portion of the evening was over. "What'll you have?" he asked Lauren.

"I'll take a pale ale. Whatever's on tap."

Ethan nodded to the waitress, who hurried off to fill their order. "So which of my many qualities clued you in?" Apparently, he wasn't letting her off that easily.

"Total honesty?"

"Absolutely." He was way too amused.

"Your stubbornness, your absolute belief you know best, and your need to take charge."

"Fair enough." Ethan thanked the waitress as she delivered the drinks.

"A quarterback is like a center on a hockey team. A good athlete is a good athlete whether he's on skates, throwing a football, or hitting a baseball." Lauren sipped the cold brew, savoring the taste as it slid down her throat. She loved a good beer.

"My thoughts exactly. But each sport requires different talents."

"You don't think you could take an outstanding football player and turn him into a hockey player?"

"I'm guessing I could." He shrugged. "If I were a hockey guy."

"Touché," Lauren snorted and took a long pull on the cold beer.

Ethan raised his beer to her in a friendly salute, his blue eyes shining with pure mischief. God, he was incredible. Absolutely incredible and so unlike any other guy she'd ever hung out with, and he respected her opinions.

Lauren enjoyed their current conversation too much to drop it. "Look at Cooper, for instance. He's our team captain, a take-charge guy, big enough to intimidate and fast on his skates. There's no one faster. He could've played other sports but he chose hockey."

Ethan rubbed his chin. "Or hockey chose him."

"What do you mean?"

"When you have the passion, it chooses you. You can't stop it any more than you can stop breathing. If you're one of the lucky ones, you take that passion to its highest level. If you're not, you become a fan, and you live through those guys on the rink or on the field."

"Spoken like a man with a true passion." She stared at him, feeling as if she'd just been given some insight into him, even as she rejected what he was not-so subtly telling her. "And hockey is your passion?"

"Sports are my passion. Purely as a spectator. Of course, as you continue to point out, I didn't grow up with a stick in my hands, and I have a lot to learn. That's where you come in."

Lauren absorbed this information as reality dawned on her. "They're going to make a spot for you in their organization, aren't they?"

The smile wavered on his face and those shutters dropped over his eyes. "It's possible. Nothing is off the table."

"You aren't just gathering information for potential owners, you're building your resume."

He relaxed against the back of the booth and rubbed his stubbled chin. The man didn't appear to own a razor, and it was sexy as hell. "Lauren, a savvy businessman is always looking over the horizon for the next challenge."

She didn't bat an eye, just studied him and wished she could read his thoughts. "Lots of savvy businessmen don't care who they step on to get what they want."

"I won't lie to you. I've been accused of that a time or two."

"And in this situation?"

"I want what's best for the team and the potential ownership." He stared her in the eyes, and for the first time, she knew he was being one-hundred-percent honest with her.

"Why come across as someone who doesn't know hockey when you're a fan?"

"I never said I didn't know hockey, never said I wasn't a fan. You made those assumptions, not me." He almost smiled. She hated it when he smiled because it changed the hard lines of his face and sucked her deeper into this spell he'd woven around her.

"You got me there," she conceded.

"I don't have an insider's knowledge, and that's where you

35

come in."

"Okay." She hedged, unsure she wanted to be his insider, depending on what he did with that info.

"Lauren, whatever happens, getting the Sleezers out of the league will be the best thing that could ever happen to this team, short of winning the Cup."

She couldn't argue with that. Back when Mr. Sleezer was alive, things weren't so bad, even though the guy was a cheap bastard, but his sons didn't have their father's work ethic or business savvy. None of the good free agents wanted to play for the Sleezers unless they broke the bank on their contract offer, and the Sleezers wouldn't do that. It'd cut into their play money. As a result, the team had to use home-grown talent and draft picks to field a decent team. Cooper Black, their star, could've gone elsewhere over the years, but he stayed out of loyalty to the city, the management, and the team, and in spite of the Sleezers. At least he'd been lucky enough to sign a pretty lucrative seven-year deal just before the old man died, making him a free agent after next season. The sons would've never paid their top player that well.

"I need you, Lauren," Ethan implored, and his quiet voice sent chills through her. As if to drive home his point, he reached across the table and grabbed her hand, his sky-blue eyes shining with the intensity of a man on a mission. For a moment, Lauren savored the feel of her hand in his. He ran his calloused thumb in small circles around her palm, and she suppressed a shudder. His eyes held hers and wouldn't let her go.

"Do you want another beer?"

The waitress's comment snapped Lauren from her dangerous thoughts and back to solid ground. She yanked her hand away.

"No, we'll take the bill." Ethan paused and sent a questioning look Lauren's way. "Unless you'd like another one?"

Lauren shot to her feet. "No, no, thanks. I need to go."

Before he could respond, she scurried away like a scared little mouse, so unlike her. She could mix it up with the roughest, toughest male but this secretive businessman sent her spinning into the boards.

She glanced over her shoulder. He was staring after her, scratching his chin thoughtfully.

Lauren got the hell out of there. She'd been swept along by the sheer force of his charisma. That just would not be tolerated. Today, tomorrow, or any day in between.

* * * *

"What a dick." Cooper growled, in a bad mood after the playoff loss. That asshole Williams invading their locker room as if he had a right drove Cooper into enforcer mode.

"So? He's a dick. We've worked for dicks most of our professional career. What's changed?" Cedric, his roommate on road trips, stretched out on his hotel room bed and tapped a text on his cell, most likely to one of the hordes of puck bunnies who followed him wherever he went.

"I don't trust him."

"I don't trust any of them, but they don't pay me to trust them. I ignore all that management bullshit. You should, too." "I just want to play hockey."

Cedric snorted. "If only it were that simple, my friend."

"What's his story with Lauren?"

"Why do you always look for ulterior motives? She's working with him, as mandated by the league, simple as that. Hell, haven't you noticed how the good ol' boys' who run this team treat her like a glorified secretary and never give her credit for anything?"

"Yeah, it pisses me off. She might be a woman, but she knows her hockey."

"Well, Ethan seems to listen to her."

"You've noticed that?"

"I notice everything. Nothing gets past these eagle eyes." Cedric leaned back against a stack of pillows, flipping through channels.

"And here I thought you were just a pretty face."

Cedric chucked a pillow at him and pegged him in the head. "Better work on your reflexes, Coop, or Dog will nail your ass in the next game." Dog Colphan was Montreal's enforcer, and he seemed to have a personal grudge against Cooper, but then most guys like him did. Cooper was that good.

Cooper threw a pillow at Cedric which glanced off his shoulder and launched a flurry of pillows around the room, but the flying pillows were interrupted by pounding. Loud pounding. Incessant pounding on the door could only mean one thing.

Cooper sighed and opened the door before the jerk woke the entire floor. Brick, their goalie, strutted in, holding a pizza box high over his head and followed by his partner in crime Alex Markov, known as Rush by all his teammates. The two young guys couldn't possibly go to sleep like the rest of the team. Brick sat the box down on the small table in the room with a flourish and a bow.

Cooper rolled his eyes, but Cedric dove for the pizza, kicking pillows out of his way as he did so. He hefted a huge slice in each big hand.

"Don't you fuckheads know we have a curfew?" Cooper pointed out, even though it was pointless. They listened to him on the ice, but not so much off it. At least they weren't out drinking and hitting on women or even worse, getting in fights. Thank the hockey gods for small favors.

"We are hungry." Alex spoke with a thick Russian accent and rubbed his flat stomach to emphasize his words.

"What better place to break curfew than in the captain's room?" Brick grabbed a piece and slouched in a chair, propping his huge feet on the edge of Cooper's bed. The kid wore nothing but a pair of shorts. Along with the bare feet, this was his usual mode of dress everywhere but on the ice. He hated clothes and loved Florida because he could get away with wearing minimal clothing. Coop wasn't sure how Brick had ever survived growing up in rainy and cold Vancouver, BC.

Cooper sighed. As if he didn't have enough to worry about with the pending sale of the Giants and his suspicions all was not what it seemed, he also had to ride herd on these clowns. All that shit could make a man consider early retirement.

Not that Cooper would ever consider that an option.

Not until he skated around the arena with the Cup hoisted high over his head.

Chapter 4—Clipping

Rubbing the back of his neck, Ethan gazed out the window of his hotel room at the city lights. Only he didn't see them, not really. He should be thinking hockey. Instead, he was thinking Lauren. What had possessed him to grab her hand and hang onto it while they sat in the bar? He'd lost his flipping mind and then some. But Lauren brought out something in him, something disturbing, exciting, and wrong—so very wrong because whether she knew it or not, he *was* her boss, and he'd been down this very wrong road once before.

Even worse, he'd told her too much, but something about her, despite her distrust of him, drew him in and made him open his mouth. Her suspicious gaze cut right through him, as if she saw beneath all the bullshit, and Ethan hated bullshitting her, but nothing could be done about it unless he walked away and didn't emerge until after the team finished its season. Only that wasn't the way he rolled. He was too hands-on, too anxious to get a handle on what he had and didn't have. He was several steps behind the league's other owners, and he was sprinting to catch up.

Ethan's instincts had served him well over the years. He often listened to them, but only after he gathered his facts. He needed those facts to substantiate the decisions his gut told him to make. Yeah, he was justifying his subterfuge ten ways to Sunday.

He was a take-charge guy, who wasn't allowed to take charge.

The team had the day off tomorrow and played another game in Montreal on Friday before flying home for the third of seven playoff games in the first round. The playoffs consisted of a best of seven series with four rounds before the final two teams played for the big prize—the Stanley Cup. There wasn't a more coveted prize in all of hockey and in Ethan's opinion, all of sports.

Brad had flown back to Seattle for a few days to do some schmoozing of politicians as they readied to break ground on the new arena and worked on all the upgrades needed to make the old arena usable for an NHL team. It barely passed muster, and the Puget Sound Hockey Alliance would be lucky to break even until they moved to the new place. His group was well aware of the issues and were all-in regardless of the risk. Ethan didn't envy Brad having to deal with Seattle politics. From where the local politicians were standing, Seattle didn't have a team yet so what was the hurry?

A panoramic view of the city of Montreal lay before him. In his biased opinion, this view didn't come close to what he saw from the windows of his historical mansion overlooking Puget Sound, in one of Seattle's most exclusive neighborhoods. It'd been in his family for over a century, and he'd been lovingly restoring it for the past two years.

Yet lately, something had been missing in his life, and he'd assumed owning a hockey team would provide the ultimate challenge and fill in the empty spaces.

Of course, his mother claimed his restlessness was due to his wandering ways when it came to women—his reluctance to settle down and raise a family. He'd never intended to be a bachelor into his thirties, but the right woman had never come along. He'd begun to wonder if his standards were too high, and he should just settle for a nice, sweet woman whose ambition centered around being a stay-at-home mom and a good wife.

Bloody hell.

That type of woman would bore him into an early grave. He liked ambitious, driven women who would never give it all up for babies and relative obscurity.

A picture of a pregnant and happy Lauren flashed through his mind. She'd been invading his thoughts a lot, though the pregnant part was a new twist. She'd make a good partner with their common interests and growing chemistry. Not to mention she had that sexy librarian thing going on. Unfortunately, she'd never trust him once he revealed his secret, and he wouldn't blame her if she kicked his ass all the way back to Seattle.

Ethan rubbed his eyes and sighed wearily. He'd always been honest in his business dealings and was proud of his well-earned rep as a straight shooter. The deception he'd been forced to perpetuate on his team weighed heavily on his conscience, and it sure as hell wouldn't get him off on the right foot with his team and staff.

He raked a hand through his hair, noting it needed a cut. Whenever he was in the middle of serious negotiations, he totally forgot about stuff like that, since his appearance didn't score high on his priority list. As a fifth generation Seattleite, he embraced flannel, jeans, and T-shirts, and like most natives, didn't own an umbrella. He loved the outdoors and exercise and hated being cooped up inside for too long. He'd have been happy doing business with loggers and shipbuilders like his ancestors had back in the 1880s.

Walking outside onto the balcony, Ethan leaned against the railing and distracted his busy mind by watching ducks circle in the pond below. The distraction didn't last long. His mind drifted back to the subject currently troubling him and perhaps the most perplexing.

Lauren Schneider.

She had a brilliant hockey mind, and like him she exuded this passion for the game that couldn't be forced. It just was.

His horny little brain slipped around a corner into a dark alley he usually avoided and wondered if that passion ran over into the bedroom. The thought of her naked and sweaty, those expressive brown eyes half-lidded and sultry, beckoned him to take a walk on the wild side with her. Ah, hell. He rubbed his hands over his face. His dick was all-in, but then no surprise there. He'd always had a healthy sex drive.

He grinned as he remembered how she'd been ready to rip him a new one when he'd gone barreling into the locker room. He almost laughed. He loved her fire and didn't hold her anger against her. In fact, he appreciated that she held the good of the team above pleasing him and the new ownership, not knowing, of course, that he was the new ownership.

Maybe his tactics had been a little high-handed, and when he took actual possession of the team, he'd never pull that crap on a coaching staff he hired. He'd trust them completely to carry out his mandate of building an NHL dynasty, because he'd settle for nothing less, and he'd force himself to have the patience to wait for it, which would be the hard part.

Ethan had his eyes on a new coach, assuming he didn't keep the existing coach, and he doubted he would. Ferrar was old school, a lot like Lauren's father, one of his senior scouts. Ethan was not. That'd be a problem, possibly an insurmountable one. Lauren, on the other hand, got it. She understood the value of the new types of statistics to measure the immeasurable. She also shared many similar opinions on the players, not that he'd been able to hear much in the way of criticism from her, but once he earned her trust, he suspected the floodgates would open.

Deserving her trust would be the hard part, especially when he was a lying bastard about his intentions and his identity, but Ethan often got what he wanted by sheer force of will. He'd do it this time, too. Sure, she'd be pissed as hell when she found out who and what he was, but she'd come around to his way of thinking when she realized how sincere he was about building this team.

Ethan's phone rang, and he walked back inside to pick it up. It was Brad. "What are you doing up?"

"Hell, the night's still young. I'm on Pacific time, remember? I haven't even gone to bed yet."

Oh, yeah, he remembered. Brad played the part of a perpetual frat guy, always looking for the next party, even at thirty-two years old. Yet the gregarious Brad was the perfect front man for the hockey ownership. Everyone loved Brad, and he won a lot more points than straight-forward, driven Ethan ever would.

"So we've got company, buddy," Brad said.

"What kind of company?" Sometimes Brad didn't make a lick of sense.

"Competition."

Ethan was getting exasperated with Brad's short answers, designed to draw out the drama. "What competition?"

"For the team."

"The team is ours."

"They don't know that, and when they find out they didn't get a chance to make an offer, all hell will bust lose."

"And I care about this why?"

Brad hesitated, most likely for emphasis and to tax Ethan's patience, which he loved to do. "A couple reasons—this other group is comprised of hockey guys who'd keep the team in Florida, and their figurehead is Lon Schneider."

"Lauren's father." Ethan absorbed this bit of information; small as it might seem, it was a potential blockbuster.

"He's a legend, and when it's announced his group has been passed over for the Seattle group, we'll be even bigger villains," Brad said.

"Shit." Ethan knew this move would be tough, but disrespecting a group of heavy-hitters like that would be a potential powder keg across the league with repercussions for years to come. Not that anyone in Seattle would give a rat's ass, but the rest of the league sure as hell would. He had so wanted to play nice with the other teams, come across as a white knight rescuing a struggling franchise. Instead he'd be the outsider yanking the team out from under a city and an ownership group with sympathy on their side.

He was surprised the commissioner had the guts to do this and hadn't mentioned the possibility of another interested party. Hopefully it was a purely political move as Ethan had the man's blessing along with the Sleezers' signatures. The league wanted hockey in Seattle, but they also wanted to look like the good guys.

Which made Ethan and his merry gang of hockey marauders the bad guys.

He'd considered the sale a done deal, except for the formalities. Now he wasn't so sure.

This binding contract might be unraveling before his eyes, and Lauren could be stuck in the middle of it all.

* * * *

Lauren couldn't sleep. She'd tossed and turned most of the night. In all her thirty years, a simple touch had never affected her like Ethan's. He'd grabbed her hand to emphasize how much he wanted her on his team, not how much he wanted her in his bed. No matter, her fertile imagination didn't need more than that to work with. Her brain took his simple gesture and elevated it to a whole new level in her dreams and her imagination.

When her phone rang at five-thirty AM, she answered it, grateful for an interruption. "Hi, Dad, what's up?" The early hour didn't alarm her. Her father often called at all hours to talk about an exciting prospect he'd found in the minors or to vent his frustrations with the latest dumb-ass move by the Sleezers.

Lon Schneider worked as the head scout for the Giants. A former NHL great, he was a shoo-in for the Hall of Fame, and the mere mention of his name opened doors wherever he went.

"Honey, tell me I misunderstood your message about possible new ownership for the team." Her father had been in Canada scouting some high school kids so he'd been out of the loop. He hated technology and rarely checked mail or answered his cell when he was heads down and sniffing out a diamond on the rink.

"It's true. The league has given the Sleezers an ultimatum. No more bailouts. They have to sell the team after the season ends."

"And they're giving some asshole the red carpet treatment because he represents an anonymous billionaire owner?"

"That's pretty much the gist of it. I've been relegated to hand-holding him." Lauren walked over to the coffee pot sitting on a stand near the dresser to start a pot of coffee. She tucked the phone under her chin.

Her father harrumphed, a sure sign he wasn't happy.

"Dad, I thought you'd be thrilled. The team could be sold to responsible ownership."

"I think the league is creating a bidding war to jack the price up."

"Bidding war? With who?" Lauren wasn't following her father.

"I've been keeping you out of the loop on this. Didn't want to get your hopes up, but I've organized a new ownership team with several deep pockets, all hockey guys, and we're making a bid for the Giants."

"What hockey guys?" Lauren went cold inside, not sure how she felt about her father's announcement.

"Me, Earl, Mike, John Carver, a few others, all guys from my playing days."

And all old school. Great guys but no great imagination or willingness to try new things, just like the current management. "Does the league know you're interested?"

"Yeah, we've been in constant contact, especially John because he's the tightest with the commish." She could tell by her father's tense tone that he was irritated. Why wouldn't he be? His group had made it known they wanted the Giants yet the league ignored them and brought in Ethan and his group? Ethan represented new blood, not necessarily a bad thing and not necessarily a good thing. Whether or not to support Ethan already tore her in two. Adding her father's group to the mix increased her confusion.

"So has John approached Commissioner Straus?"

"Not formally, but Straus is aware of us. I wanted to see what info you had before we made a formal proposal."

Figures. Her father assumed she'd choose family loyalty over team loyalty and give him any dirt she might have. The good news was that she didn't have anything useful. At least, not anythng the rest of management didn't already know. "Nothing really. The guy that's checking the team out is pretty hands-on. Asks a lot of questions."

"Who's he representing?"

"No one knows. It's all a big secret, but it came down from the top that we're to give him any information he asks for."

"If my ownership group buys the team, I could end up as GM." Her father's voice took on that tone it often did when he was driving ahead to the goal and nothing and no one would stand in his way.

"Then I couldn't work for you." Lauren thought out loud. She'd be out of a job with a team she'd given her heart and soul to for the past several years, scrabbled her way up from the bottom, always working twice as hard as any man just to prove herself.

"Of course, you could." Her father didn't seem to get it.

"Dad, it's nepotism. I couldn't work for you."

"Don't worry, honey, it's done all the time. I'll find something for you with the club." *Something* wasn't what Lauren had in mind. Not at all. She hadn't come this far to be relegated back to the clerical pool. There wouldn't be a good place for her with the Giants or anywhere else. Other teams wouldn't trust her because of her father's position. Add being a female, and she was screwed.

As always, her father disregard her concerns, which been par for the course her entire life. She'd never been Daddy's little girl, more like Daddy's afterthought. With two talented sons to follow in Lon's footsteps, he'd focused his energy on Lauren's brothers, while allowing Lauren to come along for the ride. She absorbed everything she could about hockey in an attempt to win his approval, but he barely noticed.

"So what do you know about this guy?" Her father pushed for more information, and Lauren balked, unwilling to give her personal impressions of Ethan—and not just because the jury was still out on him.

"Not much." Now that she thought about it, she spoke the absolute truth. She knew very little except he'd played college football as a quarterback. She had no idea where he was from, how old he was, how he made a living. Nothing. In fact, she didn't have a clue why a billionaire would hire this particular person to evaluate a hockey team's worth.

"You have to give me a tidbit. Something."

"Dad, he asks all the questions. He doesn't reveal a thing about himself or his employers."

"I trust you, honey. You'll do some digging for your old man, give me some leverage I can use with the league."

"I'll try." Not a chance in hell. Not now. Not while she was still figuring out whether Ethan was a good guy or bad guy.

"Good girl. I've gotta go now. Bye, hon."

"Bye, Dad. Love you." But her words were met by crickets. Lon rarely said he loved her, and she'd come to terms with that. Terms of endearment weren't his MO.

Lauren set the phone down and paced the floor. It seemed obvious to her—if the league knew about her father's group's interest, either they preferred Ethan's group, or they were attempting to drive the price up.

And somehow she'd gotten herself stuck in the middle of a possible lose-lose situation.

Chapter 5—In the Net

Ethan sat in the first row of seats in the arena, watching the Giants go through their practice routine and taking notes. Cooper Black interested him the most. He was the heart and soul of this team, loyal to a fault, a workaholic, and a passionate player. Ethan wanted nineteen more just like him. Cooper's contract was up after next season, and Ethan would do everything in his power to keep one of hockey's premier players on his ice.

Cooper skated with a mesmerizing combination of speed and athletic grace that put the most talented players to shame. Despite being thirty-two—the same age as Ethan—Cooper showed no signs of slowing down nor had he been plagued with injury problems like other players. He'd earned a reputation for toughness and resiliency, and he deserved to be on a team that did everything it could to compete for the Cup each and every year. Ethan wanted to make the Giants—soon to be christened the Sockeyes—that team and Cooper Black his cornerstone.

One problem. Black seemed to hate his guts. Dislike, Ethan could live with, but he needed the guy's respect. Ethan could schmooze and charm the best of them. With that in mind, he waited outside the locker room after practice. Cooper was the last one to leave, just like he was the first one to arrive every day.

Ethan stepped in front of Cooper, blocking his exit route. "Nice job last night. With a little more help from your offense, you'd have stood a better chance." Cooper had scored two goals, but they'd still lost.

Cooper's eyes narrowed with undisguised animosity. "What would you know about that?"

Ethan bit back a smartass retort. Getting into a pissing match with this guy wouldn't get him anywhere. "You don't care much for me, do you, Black?"

Cooper and Ethan stood the same height. Even though Ethan was no slouch, Cooper's muscles were honed from thousands of hours in the rink and the weight room. Even so, Ethan would not allow the team captain to intimidate him. He wanted Cooper on his team, not just because he had a contract but because he wanted to play for this team with this ownership in Seattle. It'd be a hard sell and a near vertical uphill climb and wouldn't happen overnight. But the first step would be to earn Cooper's respect even if the future Hall-of-Fame center hated his guts.

"Give me one good reason why I should." Cooper's chin jutted out and he clenched his jaw.

"Because we both want the same things."

"What the fuck is that?"

"To see this team become a dynasty."

"You're just here to do a job. I'm here to leave my blood, sweat, and guts on the ice—hell, my soul. I don't think guys like you even have a soul, do you, Williams?"

Ouch. Now that was low. "Souls can be bought and sold. Premier hockey players are harder to come by." Ethan smiled even though it hurt his face to do so, but Cooper's mouth retained its hard, firm line.

A muscle ticked in Cooper's jaw. "So you think I'm premier?"

"Of course, I do. I'd be a fool not to."

Cooper shrugged, not backing down and not impressed.

"Is it me you have an issue with or are you satisfied with riding the Sleezers into oblivion?"

"I hate the Sleezers. The entire team does, but I hate ownership groups who don't have the balls to reveal themselves and hide behind a thousand-dollar suit."

Ethan laughed. "Have you yet seen me in a thousand-dollar suit?"

"You know what I mean."

"I admire your honesty, even if I don't appreciate your attitude." Ethan wove steel in his voice. Black needed to know he couldn't be intimidated, and he wouldn't back down. The sooner Cooper figured that out, the sooner they could move beyond this pissing match they currently engaged in.

"You're the best, Coop, and this ownership is committed to putting the best team on the ice with you or without you."

"They haven't bought the team yet unless you know something you're not telling us."

Cooper's penetrating gaze dissected every nuance of Ethan's body language just like he dissected an opposing team's goalie and defensemen, predicting their every move. Ethan had spent years covering up his emotions, and he'd be damned if he'd give Cooper a hint of the story behind the story. Not yet.

"This team hasn't had one playoff appearance in the years since the Sleezer brothers took over the team from their father, until now. Current staff have managed to build a solid competitor with home-grown talent and young guys. But you know as well as I do that once these young guys' contracts expire, they'll come looking for their money, and the Sleezers won't pay up. You'll be back to square one."

Cooper's frown cut deeper, etching deep lines into his face, as anger flashed in his blue eyes. "I know that. I want the team sold."

"Then why are you fighting this?"

"Because something doesn't add up, and I don't trust you."

Ethan didn't respond, keeping his expression bland. This guy was too savvy, and he was one step away from figuring this whole mess out. If the sale became public before the team's last game, the deal was off, and most likely Schneider's group would get the team, and Seattle would get nothing.

That could not happen. Not on Ethan's watch. Not when he was so close he could taste it. He'd dreamed of this for so long, planned for it, waiting and watching for an opening, he couldn't lose his goal when it was within inches of his reach. Besides, he'd made a promise to his family, and Ethan took his promises seriously and so did his family. This was his contribution to the community.

Cooper scrutinized him like he was an opposing team's starting goalie. "I don't like all this secrecy bullshit. Why doesn't this group just come out and announce who they are?"

"They're not willing to do that until they've done their due diligence."

"Whatever." Cooper pushed past him and strode down the long hallway.

So much for winning over the team's best player. If anything, Ethan had dug a deeper hole for himself, and he'd raised the suspicions of the one man he didn't want sniffing around. Lauren was bad enough, especially considering who her father was.

God, he hated subterfuge. He'd always been a straightforward, honest businessman. This went against his nature.

Once the sale was announced and the move to Seattle was revealed, he wondered if any amount of damage control would repair the destruction left in their wake. Yet, he'd do it over again, knowing what he knew now because he wanted this team in Seattle that badly.

And he wanted Lauren and Cooper in Seattle along with it.

* * * *

All morning and into the afternoon, Lauren attempted to work on her stats, only she couldn't concentrate.

She wished she could dislike Ethan Williams. It'd make her life that much easier. Try as she might, her body refused to go with the program, and she wasn't sure the rest of her was buying in either. It wanted Ethan eight ways until Sunday, in the net, in the luxury suites, in the locker room showers. That horny body of hers wasn't picky. In fact, the man had lived in her dreams last night to the point where she gave up on sleep and worked on some salary cap stuff.

The Sleezers had the lowest staff and player payrolls in the league—the cheap bastards. While they wined and dined in expensive restaurants and chased around the country with models and wannabe stars, their staff held it all together, and the league bailed the Sleezers out so they could make payroll. Those days were coming to an end, which was all good. Wasn't it?

With an exasperated sigh, she sat back and sighed. Numbers weren't sticking in her head even though she'd kept at it until late afternoon, like a cat chasing its tail, round and round and getting nowhere. Ethan wanted a salary report, along with recommendations on who would be paid what if they were on a premier team. She almost smiled as she remembered his orders: *I don't deal in details. I pay staff to do that. I want a summary. I'm interested in your high-level assessment based on your data.*

Finally, Lauren headed downstairs to the hotel bar for a beer and a happy-hour appetizer. She didn't see Ethan sitting alone in a booth surrounded by messy piles of paper and numerous electronic devices until he caught her attention and waved her over. By then it was too late to cut bait and run like hell. Her feet carried her where she didn't want to go, and she slid into the booth seat across from him.

"We have to stop meeting like this." He smiled, showing off two dimples she'd never noticed before, and she was a sucker for a man with dimples, just like she was for a man with deep blue eyes, dark hair, and a long lean body. He had this one unruly lock of hair that insisted on falling over his forehead, which she found oddly sexy. Even though he wore jeans and T-shirts as opposed to business suits, he'd probably look just as at home in a suit. Today he wore his usual faded pair of jeans and a Giants sweatshirt. For a businessman, his manner of dress was curious at best, but she assumed he might be playing down his role to make the staff more comfortable around him.

He signaled to the waiter, and they ordered beers and nachos. He stacked the papers into a haphazard pile with his iPad and cell phone balanced precariously on top. Looking up, he caught her watching him and winked. "You should see my office at home."

"I'm not sure I could handle that." Lauren liked things neat and tidy, everything in its place. "A bit messy, are we?"

"Actually I like things tidy, I just pay other people to do that for me."

She nodded. That seemed to be a common theme with him. "Paying others to do the detail work for you means missing out on the journey and just arriving at the destination."

"And that's a problem?" He was still grinning, still making her heart throb. No shit, it was actually throbbing. And her panties, well, she didn't even want to think about what was going on between her legs.

"It could be because I suspect that once you arrive, you schedule another trip. You never sit back and enjoy the ride."

"Pretty much." His eyebrows furrowed, as if she'd pointed out something he hadn't considered. "My mom always tells me to stop and smell the roses because I'm too busy climbing the next mountain."

"Your mom's a smart lady. And what mountain will you tackle after this one?"

He shrugged, suddenly shutting down, his blue eyes shielded and wary. He did a quick subject change. "Ready for game two?"

"I don't have to be ready. The guys do," Lauren said. As much as she hated to say it, the few playoff series the guys played in since she'd been with the team pretty much sent her over the edge, as if she wanted something badly enough she could somehow fuel their ability to win.

It hadn't worked two nights ago.

"I'm sitting in the box tonight to get the big-picture view."

Lauren nodded. Ethan could sit anywhere he pleased. The way the league was bowing down to him, he could probably sit on the players' bench if that's what he wanted.

"I want you to join me. Any progress on the payroll stats?"

"I'm working on them. We have the lowest payroll in the league for staff and players. I can tell you that much already. That's why we lose free agents and competent staff every year. This isn't exactly a destination for elite players."

"Except Cooper."

"Yes, except Cooper. He's an anomaly. Loyal to a fault. I often wonder if he wouldn't prefer to go elsewhere."

"But he doesn't. Why is that?"

Cooper stuck around while every other decent player packed up his sticks and skated out of town at the first opportunity. "Like I said, he's loyal, which is probably not to his advantage." She thought for a few more seconds as she sipped the beer just deposited on her table. "He's done a lot of work with kids over the years at the Children's Hospital and sponsors a summer camp every year for underprivileged kids both here and in his hometown of Detroit. He's a fixture in Gainesville, lives here year round."

"A regular hero, is he?" Ethan grimaced, as if she wasn't giving him the news he wanted to hear, which made no sense.

"To a lot of people, yes, he is."

"And to you, personally, what do you think of Mr. Black?"

"Me? I think he's wonderful. He's the consummate captain, and he keeps his nose clean off the ice, which is really important when it comes to public perception. Keeps an eye on his guys, too."

Ethan nodded, rubbing his chin, a habit he appeared to have when asking the tough questions. "So, Lauren, where do you see yourself in ten years or so?"

"Doing essentially what I'm doing now." Her answer was honest and without emotion. She'd long ago accepted that she gone as high as she could in this organization, but that didn't mean she wouldn't keep fighting.

"You don't want to be the director of player personnel or the GM?"

"Of course I do, but I'm realistic, too. Don't get me wrong, I love what I do, but I'd like more responsibility, more say in how the team is built and managed. Regardless, I can't imagine doing anything else, anywhere else."

"They don't take you seriously, do they?" Obviously, he'd

noticed, not that it was difficult to figure out.

She met his gaze and shook her head.

"What if another team offered you a big salary increase?"

"What can I say? I'm loyal, like Coop. This team hired me when no one else would." She'd come running back with her tail between her legs after Max dumped her, leaving her destroyed and destitute, and begged the Giants to take her back.

"You're a rare woman, Lauren." Ethan's voice lowered an octave into that sexy range which had her body thrumming with interest, even though she wasn't sure she liked the guy. Obviously, her body had made its choice.

Kaley's words came flooding back to her. *You don't have to like a guy to screw him. It's even better if you don't because then it's all about the sex with no future expectations.*

Easy for Kaley to say. She scored in bed more than Cooper scored on the ice. Lauren rarely scored at all. She just did her job, minded her manners, and dated occasionally. She'd been burned before by a hot man with a sexy smile and a ripped body, and she'd finally learned her lesson.

Surrounded by hot hockey players from birth, it was inevitable she'd lose her virginity to one. When Lauren was sixteen, she fell head over heels for Max, one of her brother's minor league hockey teammates. He was hot. Really hot. Melt-your-panties hot. And he'd melted hers right off her. Not that she hadn't played a part. She flirted shamelessly with him until one night they'd consummated their relationship in the back seat of his old Toyota. Their torrid affair continued for a month before Max moved on to another team in another town and never looked back. Lauren was devastated. As a naïve teenager, she'd considered him her forever love, and she never completely got over him.

Years later, Max played his rookie year for the Giants, and they started where they'd left off—him, in lust and her, in love.

On a drunken whim, they flew to Vegas and married. Lauren had been in an entry-level position with the Giants, and they immediately let her go for breaking the cardinal rule—no fraternizing with the players. Max was traded to Buffalo soon after, and Lauren followed him. Within a few short months, she'd been confronted with the harsh reality. He walked out and left her bankrupt emotionally and financially before they had their one-year anniversary. So much for forever. Lauren never recovered. She'd blindly adored and trusted him. He'd betrayed her trust and stripped her of her dignity and her self-worth.

Her father convinced the Giants to hire her back, and she spent the next few years in financial and emotional recovery, going out of her way to avoid fraternizing with anyone associated with the team. Nothing would come between Lauren and her passion for hockey. She'd derailed her career once for the wrong man. She could not be that stupid again.

Ethan was such a man. The warning signs and red flags were there, only her body didn't care, it wanted him anyway, just like it had wanted Max. She tried not to listen.

If the glitter in Ethan's eyes was any indication, he was fighting his interest, too. Even if he hadn't been associated in some mysterious manner with the team, Lauren couldn't go there. He'd be out of her life in a few months, despite hints he might stay on if his ownership group purchased the team. Yet, Lauren couldn't see him sticking around. He had to have a life elsewhere, and as far as she knew, maybe a wife and kids at home, a home he never talked about. She'd been fooled before.

"Lauren?" His voice brought her back to the present.

"Sorry, thinking about the game this evening."

"Nervous?" His teasing lopsided smile caused her heart to thump a little harder against her rib cage.

"I'm always nervous before a game."

And even more so when Ethan pinned her with his intent stare and ran his fingers over his napkin as if he wished it were a specific part of her body.

Oh, God, she wished it were, too, which was all kinds of messed up.

* * * *

Cooper walked out of the locker room after a close win he didn't feel nearly as good about as he should. He hadn't scored a goal, but at least the rest of the first line picked up his slack. Cedric had played inspired hockey, all over the ice as if there were three or four of him.

Now it was back home with the series tied one-one.

Speak of the devil, Cedric stopped next to him. He followed Cooper's gaze. "You got a real issue with that guy, don't you?"

Several feet away, Ethan Williams chatted it up with the Sleezers like they were old buddies.

"The Sleezers or Williams?"

"Everybody hates the Sleezers. I was talking about Williams, our savior."

"He's not our fucking savior."

"You look like you're ready to drop the gloves every time you catch sight of Williams. Why don't you duke it out with him, get it out of your system?"

"That'd go over well with the league. They're salivating all over the guy. That's the problem, Ced. Why? If he's who he says he is, what's the big deal?"

"The big deal is the big bucks behind him. The commish trips all over himself when guys with deep pockets want to buy into the league." Cooper stiffened as Ethan threw back his head and laughed out loud at something one Sleezer said. The dick was totally faking it.

"Yeah, I know, but it's more than that. There's a damn good reason why we don't know a thing about his ownership group."

"Man, you're a distrusting soul, buddy. Let it go. Take him at face value."

"And what is that?"

"He's here to vet the team for prospective owners. Simple. To the point. As long as the Sleezers are out of our lives, what do we care, ya?" Cedric liked to throw in a *ya* once in a while to make sure everyone remembered he was from Sweden even though he didn't have much of an accent anymore.

"You'll care if they move the team."

Cedric shrugged. "Not really. I spend most of my life inside an arena. It's all the same to me wherever it is. Come the offseason, I go where I please."

"I wish I felt like you, but I'm a part of this community, and I want to keep it that way."

"Let's get to the bus. Everyone's waiting. You know how cranky Coach gets when he's tired and ready to sleep in his own bed and one of us hold up the bus."

Cooper nodded and had to laugh. "Yeah. He's already pissed at me. No reason to make it worse."

Cedric winked at a couple puck bunnies standing just outside the doorway. They squealed when they saw him, but security kept them back. He turned to Alex and Brick. "Watch and learn, children."

Cedric stopped to sign their programs. One of them wanted her chest signed, her low-cut tank not hiding much, and he gladly obliged. Cooper had to drag him away by the arm, but not before the blonde scrawled her number on a card and tucked it in his pants. Cedric grinned as she copped a feel. Cooper rolled his eyes.

Cedric loved women, and women loved him. The guy needed one of those take-a-number machines installed on the door of his condo to accommodate the steady stream of women in and out— often more than one a night or one at a time. Coop had had his share of women, and he could flirt with the best of them, but right now he was all about the playoffs.

Cedric sighed as if he were the most maligned guy on the team.

"It's the playoffs. Get your head in the game and forget about the women."

"The women are part of the game. Without the women, I wouldn't be able to wind down."

Cooper shrugged. "Whatever works, Ced."

They got the evil eye from the coach as they boarded the full bus. Cedric kicked a few young guys out of their preferred seats.

"I'm going to look into that guy," Cooper muttered for only Cedric's ears.

"What guy?" Obviously, Cedric had mentally moved on to another subject, a subject most likely with a nice rack and ass.

"Williams. I want to know his story."

"Whatever. I wouldn't put much energy into him. Whatever happens, we don't get a vote. Consider it a grand adventure." Cedric pulled his baseball cap down over his eyes and tipped his seat back, completely unconcerned.

Cooper glared at his buddy. Sometimes Cedric irritated the hell out him, but beating the crap out of the team's second highest scorer probably wasn't an option.

He sighed and stared out the window. He had good instincts, and right now his instincts didn't trust Ethan Williams.

Chapter 6—Check to the Head

The excitement of the playoffs sucked Ethan in like nothing ever had in his life—not even making his first billion on a gamble came close to the euphoria of watching *his* team win a playoff game, and they were his team—damn it.

He was walking on air after the Giants split the next two at home, losing the first and winning the second, tying the series at two-two. The playoff atmosphere in the finally sold-out arena didn't match the din of Montreal's arena, but he'd take it. For now.

Lauren had cast several strange looks at him during those games even as she was jumping up and down and screaming her lungs out. Maybe he'd been a little too excited for a guy who supposedly didn't have a horse in this race and hadn't been around long enough to develop an affinity for the staff and players or to feel part of the team.

Ah, Lauren.

Somehow, he'd managed to keep it strictly business between them even though his dick protested like a mother, and the rest of his body joined in on the torture. He could not and would not go down that road again. His family and his partners counted on him to maintain a professional attitude, and screwing one of his personnel didn't exactly breed confidence in his abilities, especially since the incident with a female employee a few years ago which ended in near disastrous consequences for the family business.

Technically no one knew he owned the team, and the staff still worked for the Sleezers. But the justifications he'd worked over and over in his head still didn't make it right.

None of his arguments wiped out his more-than-professional interest in Lauren. She intrigued him, like a sexy librarian. Sexy as hell, her hockey knowledge alone gave him a raging hard-on. Throw in her cute body, pretty face, and take-no-prisoners attitude, and he was all in, even though he couldn't be. He needed her as an employee, and a temporary fling would change their relationship irrevocably. In addition, he was slowly earning her trust, even though on so many levels, he didn't deserve it.

Tonight they were back in Montreal and sat in the guest owner's box. Conspicuously absent were the Sleezers. Relieved, Ethan didn't miss for an instant the constant bickering and whining of the brothers and their ladies du jour.

Lauren looked around the small box then at Ethan. "Where is everyone?"

"I haven't a clue. It's like we missed an important memo or something." Ethan popped the tops on two beers from the small bar in the corner of the room. "Might as well avail ourselves of the perks."

"I like nothing better than spending the Sleezers' money." She quipped and smiled tentatively at him. His heart did this little thump-thump which had become par for the course around her lately. She was dressed uncharacteristically in a Giants jersey and a pair of jeans, her long, silky milk-chocolate hair tied in a sassy, though neat, ponytail rather than her usual prim bun. Ethan like sassy. Hell, he just liked her. Too much.

"Coop's not having the best series." Ethan commented, trying to distract his libido, but not even hockey could do that.

"Coach is playing him too much, not giving him a chance to rest his legs. He's no good to us tired. This team has other guys who can skate, but Coach is too conservative, too afraid to give them their shot."

"I was thinking that myself." Ethan hadn't been overly impressed with Fur so far. When the team lost, they lost because of the man's decisions, the matchups he put on the ice, his game management, and when they won, they won in spite of him. Or so it seemed to Ethan, but he needed more information.

He glanced at Lauren. She sucked her lower lip into her mouth and chewed on it. He took a long pull on his beer to stop himself from groaning. Instead he choked.

"Are you all right?" She studied him with concerned brown eyes.

"I'm fine, I just—just. Nothing."

Lauren fidgeted, her hands primly in her lap. "I don't mean to say Coach isn't good, but he tries too hard sometimes. He's a great coach. We're so lucky to have him." She rushed to correct her statements by doing damage control, probably afraid she'd said too much.

"Don't worry, Lauren. Your opinions are safe with me." Yeah, right, like he didn't have the power to turn this team on its head and spin it. And he most likely would. The information she fed him in bits and pieces became part of the bigger puzzle being worked out in his brain.

"I don't want to criticize anyone. I'm not in his position, so it's not fair of me to second-guess his decisions. Too many other people are doing that."

"I understand." What the hell else could he say? That the coach was most likely on the hot seat? That he already had his eye on the guy's successor, a fiery, young, progressive assistant coach for a perpetual playoff team who'd be a hot item once the playoffs ended.

Ethan stared down at the ice. The skaters circled and weaved during their warm-ups, somewhat reminding him of hawks circling over a clearing while on the hunt. These guys had the same grace and fluid motion, and he never got tired of watching them.

He never got tired of watching Lauren, either, especially when she didn't know he was. He loved how she leaned forward and grabbed the seat in front of her during the game, her face an intense study in concentration. She didn't hold back when she saw a bad call. She called out her guys when they screwed up—not that they could hear her—and she literally jumped up and down in her seat when they executed a perfect pass or defensive move that stopped a score.

God, he loved so many things about her in such a short amount of time and keeping their relationship strictly business was killing him, especially when she cast longing glances at him through lowered lashes. That definitely killed him.

Regardless, he was here for hockey, not for any other reason.

* * * *

Lauren sat in her office the next morning after four hours of sleep, her fingers wrapped around a strong cup of French Roast coffee.

They'd flown back to Florida late last night after winning game five in Montreal. Coop had been on fire, and the Giants won by a score of 2-1. One more win and they'd advance to round two. Wow. Imagine that. Round two of the playoffs for a team not predicted to make the playoffs. Cooper and Cedric carried the team on their broad shoulders and inspired their young goaltender to reach new heights. Brick possessed this unique instinct, prized in goalies, of knowing where the puck was heading before the shot was taken. He'd made a few mistakes, but not a lot.

She was exhausted, but sleep hadn't been an option. She couldn't stop all the thoughts ping-ponging around in her brain—Ethan, Cooper, the team, her father, and everything else revolving around her current situation, most of which started and ended with Ethan.

She had misgivings, but she wanted to trust him. His enthusiasm for the team contradicted his story that he was just a middle man for the nameless/faceless billionaires who'd control this team's fate. Something just didn't add up. Regardless, no one could be worse than the Sleezers, and she constantly reminded herself of the fact. Unless they uprooted the team.

Rubbing her bloodshot eyes, she stared at the headlines on the hockey sites. The wildcard Giants were gaining the attention of the entire NHL. Everyone liked an underdog.

Kaley waltzed into Lauren's office and dropped some mail on her desk. "Great game last night, huh?"

"Oh, yeah. Incredible." Lauren sat back and massaged her neck, but nothing eased the tension. "How have things been here?"

Concern flashed in Kaley's eyes and put Lauren on instant alert. Lauren sat up quickly. "What is it?"

Kaley didn't look her in the eye. Instead she stacked and restacked the mail into a tidy, little pile.

Alarm rose in Lauren. Kaley didn't usually let shit get to her, yet something obviously had.

Her friend abandoned the pile of mail and met Lauren's gaze. "I picked up Brad at the airport last night."

"You didn't sleep with him, did you?" Lauren shook her head and sighed, almost relieved it wasn't anything more serious.

"No, it's not that—not that I didn't want to rip his clothes off and jump him right there on the luggage carousel, but no, I didn't."

"Then what is it?" Lauren's fears flooded back, fears she'd been holding at bay since that morning they'd been told to play nice with Ethan.

Kaley turned around to shut Lauren's door. She sat down in the seat next to Lauren and leaned forward, keeping her voice a whisper. "What do you know about Brad and Ethan? Who are they really? Where are they from?"

Lauren thought for a moment, realizing she didn't know a thing. "It's never come up, and it's none of my business."

"Did you assume they were from the east coast, at least?"

Lauren nodded slowly. "Well, yeah." Her stomach clenched as she fought back a wave of nausea. *Please, dear God, no.*

Kaley's red lips pulled in a thin, grim line. She glanced around the room as if it were bugged, then whispered. "Brad's plane flew in from Seattle."

"Seattle?" A metallic taste filled Lauren's mouth. She swallowed and got a grip on her emotions. Not Seattle. Not the very city stalking every NHL team with crappy ownership and in a tenuous position, like the Giants. Especially the Giants.

"When I asked him about it, he blew it off, mumbled something about being in Seattle for business."

"I'm sure that's all it is." Lauren didn't believe her own words. Everything made sense, the deception, the secrecy, the mandate from the league that Ethan be given any information and access he required. Who was Ethan Williams? Really, who the hell was he? She'd Google him the first chance she got. And Brad? What the hell was Brad's last name?

"I hope you're right, but it did put a damper on getting any from Brad. He was anxious to go straight to his hotel, as if he couldn't wait to get away from me."

And her prying eyes, no doubt.

"What's Brad's last name again?"

"Reese, I think." Kaley shrugged, all serious with none of her usual diva-may-care attitude. "I just thought you might want to know."

"Thanks. Not sure what to make of it. My dad has similar concerns. He wants me to spy on Ethan, get some dirt. Dad's part of another potential ownership group vying for this team."

"What are you going to do?"

"My job. Right now the league has mandated we help Ethan so that's what I'll do." Lauren sounded braver than she felt.

"I'm glad I'm not in your shoes." Kaley headed for the door. Hand on the doorknob, she hesitated. "Lauren?"

Lauren glanced up from her computer screen. "Yes?"

"Don't get burned."

"Burned? By Ethan?"

"Of course, by Ethan. He has it bad for you, and you do for him."

"You noticed?" Lauren didn't attempt to deny it. Kaley saw through her as easily is if she were a window.

"It's pretty obvious, but I know you."

"I don't get emotionally attached. Not anymore. I learned my lesson about sleeping with a player—on and off the ice."

"Just be careful. This guy is a heartbreaker." On that note, Kaley left her office, deserting Lauren and leaving her alone with her thoughts—disturbing thoughts that Ethan might well be screwing them all over, most of all her.

And, yes, that would break her heart, and she wasn't sure her fragile heart could take another hit.

* * * *

When Ethan walked into Lauren's office that morning, she appeared to be waiting for him, and whatever was on her mind wasn't good. He tried a disarming smile. If her scowl was any indication, she'd reloaded instead of being disarmed.

He slid into the chair next to her desk and leaned back in a casual pose, clasping his hands in front of him, fingers linked. "Great game last night. We just need one more win. The guys are playing their hearts out."

"We?"

Her response caught him off-guard and could be interpreted a dozen different ways. "Uh, yeah, we. I feel as if I'm a part of this team. Cooper and Cedric are playing the best hockey I've seen, and I couldn't ask for more from Brick."

She studied him suspiciously and said nothing, not even hockey talk changed her attitude this morning. He leaned forward, studying her closely. "Did I piss you off or something?"

Eyes blazing, she shot out of her chair, fists clenched, and started pacing the floor of her small office. Two steps down, two steps back. Damn, but she was attractive when she was pissed, all hot and passionate. About what he hadn't a frigging clue, but it definitely had to do with him. Her passion definitely turned him on, and it definitely should not and could not.

Ethan, a man of action, forced himself not to take action and wait her out, even though her agitation made him nervous and fear the worst.

Lauren stopped her pacing to stand before him, hands on hips, shoulders back defiantly, and gorgeous breasts pushed out. His gaze momentarily dropped to her chest, his mouth watered, and he licked his lips, swallowing hard. He forced his gaze back to her face, her very angry, very hurt face. Her eyes searched his as if probing for a truth he couldn't give.

"Who *are* you, Ethan Williams?" Her voice rose with each syllable.

"I'm not sure what you're getting at?" Ethan forced his face into an expression of pure innocence, faking his confusion, while his guts churned in a tsunami of regret that he couldn't be honest with her.

"Don't play dumb with me. Where are you from? Where do you live?"

"I don't see how that's relevant." Ethan's brain raced ahead, working on a way out of this. He couldn't give her what she wanted, not with the league's gag order and not without endangering his precarious grip on this team.

"Oh, but it is, it's very relevant. Especially if the answer is Seattle." Her eyes narrowed as they lasered into his.

Ethan's heart did a nose dive. He hated lying. Absolutely fucking hated it. He stood, needing his height advantage in this battle of wills. "Seattle? Where it rains all the time? I have residences in a few places. In fact, Seattle in the summer is the most beautiful place on earth." Everything he said was the truth, albeit a little skewed.

"What other places do you have residences? In Florida, by chance?"

"Of course." Did a hotel suite count? Lying went against his grain and how he liked to do business. He might have pissed off a few people with his forthrightness in the past, but they could never accuse him of being deceptive even if they didn't like his message or his actions.

Lauren studied him for several seconds, and he stared back at her with a calmness he sure as shit didn't feel. Finally she blew out a long breath and sank into her desk chair. "You wanted to see a summary of salary comparisons between our lines and the rest of the league. Here they are."

Grateful to be back to the task on hand, Ethan gladly moved to stand behind her desk. He leaned down to study her computer screen and breathed in the fresh scent of something spicy, like a sassy perfume meant for an outdoors type girl. He'd love to take her hiking in the Olympic Mountains or for a walk along the shoreline at Alki Beach or sailing on Puget Sound. If she gave the Pacific Northwest a chance, she'd love it there.

Ethan leaned closer—he couldn't resist—his head next to hers. Just a few inches and they'd be kissing, and kissing her definitely appealed to him. Her fiery confrontation had excited him, pushed some of his severely taxed caution to the point of no return.

Lauren's hand shook on the mouse. He suppressed a smile, feeling pretty damn smug she was as susceptible to him as he was to her. No one should go through this torture alone.

Somehow he'd convince her to come to Seattle with him, once he could tell her he was moving the team, and if she didn't castrate him when she found out about his deception. He chuckled out loud. He expected nothing less from her.

"What's so amusing?" She tilted her head, leaning away from him, and looking up to meet his gaze. Ethan sucked in a breath. She was so damned alluring.

Needing to break the spell, he walked to her window, hands clasped behind his back so she couldn't see how bat-shit crazy she made him. "Remind me later to share with you."

Lauren couldn't seem to let well enough alone. In seconds she stood next to him, staring out the same window, seeing the same things with her eyes, but most likely seeing them very differently.

A lock of her tidy brown hair escaped from her bun and fell across her cheek. She reached up to brush it away, but Ethan caught her hand to stop her in a purely spontaneous reaction. With his free hand, he tucked her hair behind her ear and smiled. She smiled up at him, and her lips parted in that age-old silent invitation to be kissed.

He wanted to kiss her in the worst way, and despite all the reasons he shouldn't, he couldn't resist. He dropped her hand and framed her face in his hands, stroking her high cheekbones with his index fingers. She shivered but made no move to get away.

"Ethan," she whispered in a sexy, throaty whisper which sent a rush of lust to his groin.

"Lauren," he responded, his own voice raspy.

She stared into his eyes, her hazel eyes troubled and full of earnest questions, most likely fueled by her suspicions, which were well founded. Ethan held his breath, sensing another tough question coming his way.

"Is your primary residence in Seattle?"

He couldn't lie again, just couldn't. So he did the only thing he could think of to change the subject and give her something else to fixate on.

He kissed her.

Oh, yeah, he kissed her. He intended for it to be a brush of the lips, enough to distract her. But her eyes glazed over, and she closed them just as his lips touched hers. Warning bells clanged in his head and he silenced them mentally without effort, a testament to how committed he was to doing the wrong thing because it felt so right.

Her kiss tasted like warm, soft rain on a Seattle summer day and lapped at the corners of his soul like gentle waves across the sandy beach below his home. He felt as lightheaded as a teenager experiencing those first heady emotions of a new love. But this was not love and Ethan was no teenager and neither was Lauren. She was an adult woman, and he was a man, and this man wasn't strong enough to resist.

Lauren made a sound halfway between a purr and a whimper and grasped his shoulders. He ran his tongue across the seam of her lips, and she immediately opened for him. Ethan slipped his tongue inside, tasting, touching, dancing. He pulled her closer, their bodies pressed against each other. Lauren snaked her arms around his neck, and she kissed him as passionately as he'd kissed her, as if they hadn't a concern in the world.

And they had plenty of concerns. None of which Ethan gave a shit about at the moment. Instead he buried his fingers in her silky hair and deepened the kiss.

"Lauren?" Kaley rapped on the office door.

"Damn," they muttered in unison a split second before they shot apart as if they'd been shocked by a Taser. Lauren's cheeks were flushed, her bun lopsided, and she tugged her shirt to smooth out the wrinkles then patted a hand on her messed-up bun.

"Lauren? Can you take a call?" Kaley spoke again from behind the closed door.

Lauren swallowed and cleared her throat, visibly composing herself. "Ethan and I are working on a project. Take a message, please."

Silence for a moment, and Ethan knew they hadn't fooled Kaley one bit. "Okay."

Lauren turned to Ethan, her face reflecting an array of conflicting emotions. "We shouldn't have done that. I'm sorry."

"I'm not," Ethan said with total honesty. He might be forced to lie about everything else, but he'd be damned if he'd lie about the kiss.

"But we shouldn't be doing this."

"I know, but we did, and I don't regret it. Maybe it's not the best idea. For the record, I don't normally come on to women I work with." Except for that one dumbass mistake.

"I don't either."

"Come on to women you work with?" He grinned, lightening the tone.

"You know what I mean." She smiled, too, and it lit up her face, removing some of the worry lines.

"I do."

"Ethan, seriously, we can't do this." She glanced at the door, probably mentally cataloguing how many people on the other side of that door suspected what was going on.

"I know." He meant it. He just wasn't sure if he could do it.

"We have to keep our relationship totally business."

"Totally business."

"We're colleagues, in a sense."

"Absolutely, colleagues."

"And we'll keep it strictly professional from now on."

"Strictly professional."

"Would you stop repeating me?"

He chuckled, breaking through her earlier discomfort after the kiss. "It won't happen again." As long as she didn't mention Seattle—if she did, all bets were off. He'd kiss the hell out of her to keep from answering the Seattle question and to postpone seeing the inevitable pain of betrayal in her expressive eyes. He didn't want to be a lying jerk in her book. He wanted to be the hero, but fat chance that'd happen. Not once she knew the truth.

She slipped into her cool businesswoman mode. "We need to get back to work. About those salaries. I'll send the report to you, and you can go over it on your iPad."

Ethan nodded, retreating to his office space, feeling like a kid who'd been scolded by his teacher. Wicked thoughts of Lauren dressed as a teacher complete with a paddle and sexy glasses instantly came to mind.

Crap, this had to stop.

He ran his fingers through his hair and sighed, opening the report, and staring at the numbers swimming on the screen.

As if he'd be able to concentrate.

Chapter 7—Face Off

For the next week, Lauren pretended as if nothing had happened between Ethan and her, no panty-melting kiss, no shiver at the mere mention of his name, no late-night dreams starring a certain gorgeous businessman. On the inside, she knew better. She was a hot mess of mixed emotions, misplaced loyalties, and nagging uncertainties. Ethan, meanwhile, behaved as if it never happened. *Never.* A guy as sexy, gorgeous, and most likely rich as him probably kissed women so frequently that he didn't consider their little kiss a big deal.

Lauren did.

In fact, she struggled with the comparisons to her ex-husband. He, too, had been secretive and mysterious, obviously traits which attracted her. Max had been a handsome, charming man who knew what he wanted and went for it. Once he got what he wanted, he moved on to something or someone else. Lauren had been stupid enough to believe he'd loved her. Despite all the warnings of friends and family about Max's liaisons with puck bunnies while on road trips, she'd staunchly stuck her head in the sand. Until that fateful night, she shown up at his hotel room to surprise him for his birthday. Oh, yeah, she'd been surprised all right. So had the three naked women occupying his bed with him. Max, on the other hand, didn't seem the least bit fazed and immediately told her, in front of those naked women, he wanted a divorce.

You're boring, unattractive, and I want out, he'd stated with no more emotion than he showed when ordering a drink in a bar.

His words devastated her. His infidelities destroyed her. And the break-up ruined her faith in her ability to judge a person's character. She thought it couldn't get worse, but it did. That fatal night had only been the beginning of her nightmare. She was still putting her pieces back together six years later. She couldn't take another shot like that with a mysterious man, and Ethan fit the description perfectly.

She so did not need a man in her life, at least not a serious relationship with one. Hockey was her life, and the only life she needed. Thank God for hockey.

The wildcard Giants had won the next one at home, and Cooper played like the Hall-of-Famer he was certain to be. He scored two goals and had three assists, even blocking shots on defense. He elevated his play to a new level and the team followed. The win advanced the Giants to the second round, and the Sleezers suddenly took notice—unfortunately. Attention whores and opportunists, they conducted interviews, waxing poetic about how they were the stewards of their father's vision. Lauren wanted to puke.

Ethan never commented on the Sleezers, maintaining a politically correct and polite relationship with the worthless brothers. They, in turn, catered to Ethan, as if they owed him something. It was strange, and Lauren wasn't the only one who noticed. In fact, her father tried to corner her several times, but she managed to slip past him.

Lauren wasn't so lucky this afternoon. She walked into the long concrete hallway outside of the locker room just before game one of the quarter-finals in New York. Her father walked out of the visiting coach's office and stopped, waiting for her.

"You've been avoiding me." Leave it to Dad to get straight to the point, reminding her of another infuriating man in her life.

"I've been busy." She couldn't bring herself to meet his gaze, feeling as if her close association with Ethan betrayed her father.

"Coach is worried."

"About the team? They seem to be in a groove; I would think he'd be flying high." Lauren glanced around for a reason to escape.

"He's worried about the Sleezers, the sale—something seems out of whack."

Lauren chewed on her lower lip and stalled. Something did seem out of whack, and in the past, she'd discussed stuff like this with her father. She held back this time through a possible misplaced loyalty to Ethan, torn between the two men and not knowing where she stood.

Ethan took her seriously and respected her opinions, which was more than she could say for the men managing this organization. It felt good to be given credit for her knowledge. The others discounted what she said because Number One she was young, and Number Two she was a woman. She'd make a suggestion, and they wouldn't hear her. A few minutes later a man would make the same suggestion and they'd declare him brilliant.

So, yeah, maybe she did owe a little loyalty to a man who listened and actually gave her credit for her knowledge and hard work.

"I'm sure Coach doesn't have a thing to worry about." As a member of the good ol' boys' network, he didn't strike Lauren as the type of coach Ethan would want on staff, but then Ethan wouldn't be making those decisions. Surely new ownership would keep the current GM, but then he wasn't even as progressive as Coach, and that was saying a hell of a lot.

Her father narrowed his eyes and studied her. "And you know this how?"

"I don't know at all, but I doubt the new owners will clean house until they evaluate what they have."

"Isn't that what your friend Ethan is doing here?"

"Ethan is not my friend. I've been told to work with him so I am. It's my job."

"It's your job to be loyal to the team and the staff who gave you a shot when no one else would. Don't forget that, Lauren. Don't let some handsome bastard destroy your good sense."

Lauren bristled and bit back a smart-mouth retort. "Dad, don't worry about me. I've always been the practical, clinical one, except for one lapse in judgment, and I learned my lesson."

"I know you'll do what's good for the team and for hockey. You have the same passion for it as the boys, much to your mother's disgust," her father said, laying on the guilt trip.

Lauren did have an affinity for the game, a fact which still made her mother cringe. She hated hockey, hated the violence, and hated the fact that her daughter embraced hockey with a passion to equal the male members of the family. Her mom had never forgiven Lauren for following her father and brothers into hockey, which probably contributed to why Lauren seldom saw her. If Mom wasn't bitching about hockey, she was bitching about Lauren's father to the point where she'd forced each of her children to pick between their parents. They'd all picked Dad over a mother who partied like a college kid and never grew out of it. Last Lauren heard, she was living in Vegas and dating a limo driver half her age.

Aunt Jo, their father's sister, had come to live with them after the divorce. She raised them while their dad traveled on road trips. Aunt Jo was gay, but her girlfriend, a prominent doctor, stayed firmly entrenched in the closet so Jo lived with the Schneiders and snuck to secret rendezvous with the love of her life.

Aunt Jo loved hockey as much as the men in the family and taught Lauren a lot about it. Their mother was appalled that her children were being raised by "that" woman. Since she didn't want the responsibility of raising children herself, her bitching didn't carry any threat to their odd little family.

Lauren hadn't exactly been raised to be a girlie girl, but thanks to a college roommate, she'd picked up the finer points of makeup and clothes. Ethan, who obviously knew how to hang with the rich and famous, could slum with the best of them in his worn jeans and ratty T-shirts. She envied and admired the confidence it took to not care about what others thought while she had to dress the part to gain even a smidgen of respect.

Damn, lately every thought she had circled back to Ethan. Just yesterday she was thinking about whether or not to get a latte or an espresso, and she wondered which Ethan would pick. This morning in the shower she wondered what kind of soap he preferred—a regular bar of soap or some frou-frou stuff.

Her father snapped his fingers in front of her face. "Hey, pumpkin, where did you go?"

"Nothing, just thinking about Aunt Jo, wondering how she is. Have you heard from her lately?"

"No, not in a month or so. I'm guessing she's busy. We'll hear from her eventually. We always do." Her father met her gaze, his own troubled, and Lauren felt a twinge of guilt, knowing she was hiding stuff from him—her own father, the man who'd do anything for his little girl if it wasn't hockey season and her brothers didn't need him.

"Lauren, what do you hear from your mother?"

"Nothing. She's off with her latest boy toy. Last I heard they were living in Vegas, bartending while he drives a limo."

"Figures." Lon muttered. "What about the Sleezers and Williams' group?"

"Nothing's changed."

"Nothing?"

"Absolutely nothing. What about your group?"

"They're in conversations with the commissioner, not sure it's getting anywhere. He's being evasive."

"Nothing new there." Lauren frowned, recalling Kaley's report of Brad flying in from Seattle. "Have you heard any gossip on the

Seattle group?"

Lon frowned. "Not a damn thing, which worries me. I expected them to be all over the Giants, but they're oddly quiet. Something's not as it seems."

Lauren shrugged, pushing aside a seed of doubt which had grown into a thorny plant.

"Do some digging for me. Find out if Ethan is on the up and up. I want to know what his story is."

"Dad, he's pretty closemouthed."

"You're clever, Lauren. Trick it out of him." Lon waved at the coach as he walked by.

"I'm counting on you," he called over his shoulder as he caught up with Coach. The two men bent their heads together as they walked down the long hallway and out the double doors.

Lauren stared after them and wondered what the hell to do. Did she have the guts to dig for the information her father wanted, and did she even want to know the truth?

* * * *

Waiting for the first game of the second round in New York, Ethan glanced at his watch and resisted the urge to pace in the owners' box.

The Sleezers weren't there yet, thank God, but it wasn't the Sleezers he was worried about. Where the hell was Lauren? Usually she beat him to the box, and he'd find her tapping away on her tablet, taking notes, and watching warm-ups to see who seemed on and who seemed off. But tonight she was conspicuously absent, and her absence bothered him.

He needed her grounding presence because right now he was anything but grounded. He was a ship cast adrift and floating away from shore.

Lately, it was Brad and him against the world, or at least the league. Something was up with the Sleezers, and based on the murmurings he'd heard about a group headed by Lauren's father, Ethan feared his agreement didn't amount to a cup of coffee until he had the team packed up and moved to Seattle. Without the league's final blessing, any agreement wouldn't be worth the paper it was printed on. The Sleezers could be true to their name and sell out to the highest bidder.

Fine, he could play hard ball and match them penny for penny. Only he couldn't do a damn thing about a team playing above their abilities and a city who had suddenly rallied around them. Public opinion mattered, as long as the cash backed it up. The league would rather keep a team where it was if the support was there.

Then there was Lauren. Hell, he couldn't banish that one kiss from his mind. Even worse, as much as he should regret his impulsive action, he didn't, not one bit. She'd felt too good, too soft and pliable in his arms. A guy couldn't regret something like that no matter how stupid it might be for a business standpoint, the very line of thinking which had gotten him into trouble in the past.

And where did Lauren figure into all this team turmoil? Where did her loyalties lie? Was she a spy for the other side? Just when he was beginning to trust her and she trust him, those doubts started gnawing away at their fragile faith. Not that he deserved her trust, considering his deception, but he had the best interests of the team at heart and hopefully that'd count for something.

Lon was Lauren's father. He'd mounted a campaign to keep the team in town, not to mention keep his job safe and sound. Ethan couldn't guarantee job security for any of the current staff, except Lauren. She was brilliant, and the more he listened to her, the more he wanted her as part of the Sockeyes' organization.

How the hell he was going to achieve that monumental task he had no idea. He didn't possess the mountain of charm it would take to convince her to join his team once she knew the complete story. He doubted even Brad's charisma could fix this mess.

The door opened, and he jerked around to see who it was. He couldn't stop the flood of relief most likely showing on his face. "I was worried about you." The words escaped like a puck shooting across the ice.

She looked at him through lowered lashes and smiled at him as she slid into her seat. "I'm fine."

God, she was hot when she played the coy female. Ethan shrugged and fought for control. "It's just not like you to be late like this."

"My taxi got caught up in traffic. Don't worry, I can handle myself."

"I'm sure you can. It was just out of character."

Lauren's hazel eyes focused on him, and he almost fidgeted. She was his weakness. He wanted to kiss her again and take it farther until nothing separated them but skin. Hell, he'd crawl under her skin given half the chance.

Ethan blinked a few times, finding her staring at him strangely. He smiled a broad smile as if nothing was wrong. She graced him with a tentative, suspicion-laced smile. She had a right to be suspicious, and she didn't know the half of it. If only he could confide in her, gag order be damned, yet surely her loyalties would be with her father, not with him.

He couldn't blame her. He'd give anything to be able to share his vision for a hockey dynasty in the Pacific Northwest with her at his side, strictly professionally of course.

"No Sleezers?" she asked.

"Are you complaining?"

"Hell no."

Ethan chuckled. "Let's hope they don't make it."

"They'll be here if we win to hog the limelight."

Ethan shrugged. He didn't care much about the Sleezers other than whether or not the assholes might screw him over or start a bidding war in which they'd be the only winners.

He wanted this move to happen with a minimal amount of drama, but perhaps he'd underestimated the power of the other players now involved.

"So Lauren, what do you think the team's chances are tonight?" he asked casually.

Lauren shook her head. "They're playing out of their minds, like a team possessed. Inspired play, really. On paper this team doesn't have strong enough second- and third-lines to carry them this far."

"Sometimes trying and believing go further than talent."

"They do in this case."

Ethan had to smile. "You're proud of your boys, aren't you?"

Lauren turned to him, her eyes lit up with pure joy. "Yes, yes, I am. They deserve better than they get."

"Better what exactly?"

"A more loyal fan base, more progressive coaching methods to capitalize on a relatively young team and inspire them to—" She stopped and jerked her head away from him, staring at the ice. Her mortified expression telegraphed her fear of having said too much.

Ethan leaned toward her, their shoulders rubbing. "Lauren, I only want what's best for the team. You have to trust me no matter what happens or what people say."

"What do you mean *you* want what's best for the team?" She turned to him, her gaze shrewd, assessing his minor slip-up.

"I'm referring to the ownership group of which I'm a part in some small way."

"Do they really want that? Do you want that? What would you do, Ethan, to give this team the support it deserves?"

Ethan hesitated. "I'd do almost everything you've outlined to me. I'd give them the best facilities. I'd pay for the best players, and I'd hire the best support staff money could buy."

Lauren nodded and stared into his eyes. "I think you would do that, Ethan, because I suspect you don't do anything halfway."

If she only knew.

* * * *

Lauren should've said no. A smart woman would've gone back to her room and turned down Ethan's offer for a late dinner, but she was starved. At least, that was her story, and she was rocking the denial card pretty damn hard right about now.

Once back at the hotel, they headed straight for the almost empty restaurant.

The Giants won their first game against a talented New York team in front New York's hostile and rabid home crowd. After that win, she couldn't possibly sleep. She wanted to talk hockey all night long, and knew Ethan would be more than happy to accommodate her.

Lauren looked forward to their post-game analysis. Ethan was catching on. While he still asked more questions than he answered, he came up with a few good insights, which surprised and pleased her. She took a small measure of credit for his growing hockey knowledge.

Despite her best efforts, she liked Ethan, might even consider him somewhat of a friend. He was the consummate gentleman, except for that one lapse, never coming on to her and keeping everything friendly and businesslike. She couldn't stop her carnal thoughts about him, and she'd seen the fire burning in his eyes on more than one occasion.

Still there was something about him. More than once, she'd opened up her web browser intent on researching the man, and each time fear gripped her, and she couldn't follow through. Not heeding the red flags had been something she'd done back in her Max days. Now history repeated itself. Only Ethan wasn't cheating on her with another woman. She suspected he might be cheating on her city and her team, but right now she wasn't prepared for the truth.

As they walked into the restaurant, Cedric waved them over to the large table where six of the guys sat poring over menus. Lauren hesitated, but Ethan didn't. With a sigh, Lauren followed him. The man had major balls, which he'd need if he was going to attempt a buddy session with Cooper.

The team captain sat at the table, arms crossed over his chest, and his chin jutting out in a masterful display of belligerent arrogance. Ethan ignored him, obviously deciding it was wiser to focus on Coop's teammates, who didn't look nearly so annoyed and unapproachable.

The boys scooted over, leaving room for Lauren and Ethan to squeeze in between Cedric and Cooper. Lauren took the seat next to Coop to mitigate any possible bloodshed.

Ethan sat next to Cedric. It was a tight squeeze, and Lauren didn't relish being thigh-to-thigh with this sexy businessman in threadbare blue jeans. The heat from his body mingled with hers, and she gulped down a glass of water. Swallowing, she folded her napkin in her lap with a shaking hand and glanced around the table to see if anyone else had noticed.

The guys were oblivious, except for Cooper. He rubbed his jaw thoughtfully and raised one black brow. Mortified, Lauren ducked her head, while the heat rose from under her collar to her neck and face. Good thing it was dark in this corner. She chanced a second glance at Cooper. He frowned at her, his blue eyes angry and uncompromising. The man noticed everything, and he definitely noticed her reaction.

He leaned toward her and whispered in her ear. "I thought you were smarter than that."

"Smarter than what?" She played coy about as badly as Coop played nice.

Cooper rolled his eyes. "Honey, that guy's bad news. He's not what he appears to be, and you're going to get burned if you put your hand in that fire."

Boy, didn't she know it, but Coop couldn't know she knew. She smiled sweetly at him, glad Ethan was in an animated conversation with Cedric about skiing in Sweden.

"He's just doing his job, like you and I are." She defended Ethan with a completely straight face even as she perpetuated unspeakable acts on the napkin under the table.

Cooper didn't respond, just tossed her another of his calling-bullshit-on-you looks.

"Nice game, Brick," she said, turning to the goalie. He grinned at her. Martin Bricker was hell on opposing team's offenses, and off the ice, he was one crazy man, though behind the crazy persona lurked a savvy businessman. Brick hated wearing a lot of clothes, and tonight despite the cold weather, he wore shorts, a tank, and flip flops.

"Thanks, Lauren. I aim to please, eh," he said with an exaggerated Canadian accent, as he tipped an imaginary hat.

Ethan turned his head toward Brick and nodded. "Great save on that one play. You snatched that puck out of thin air and stopped a sure goal."

Brick grinned at Ethan until he caught Cooper's scowl out of the corner of his eye. The smile dropped off his face, and he stared down at the table. Ethan aimed an accusing glare at Cooper, shooting him squarely between the eyes, but Cooper didn't flinch. If anything, he smirked.

"We've won the first one, boys. Three to go boys. We can do this." Cooper addressed his teammates. They nodded and murmured agreement as the waitress served their food and everyone dug in, the conversation completely dying as the guys ate ravenously after burning all those calories in a hard-fought game.

Feeling eyes on her, Lauren glanced up. The goalie watched her plate with hungry eyes. He'd eaten everything on his plate and zeroed in on the fact she was just toying with her food.

"You gonna finish that?"

Lauren pushed her plate across the table to Brick.

"Hey, don't get your hand too close to him. He'll eat that too," Cedric joked.

The table erupted in laughter, except for Coop and Ethan. They eyed each other like two alpha dogs sizing the other up before a big fight. Ethan matched Coop glare for glare, and not many people had the guts to do that.

Pride for Ethan surged through Lauren, and she had no right to that particular emotion or the ones that made her panties wet and her palms sweat.

Chapter 8—Delayed Offside

The next week and a half was a wild ride, and Lauren hung on for all she was worth. After trading wins with New York in New York, winning two at home, and losing another in New York, the Giants squeaked out a win in game six at home and advanced to the semi-finals against Boston. Four wins stood between this unlikely team of misfits and rejects and playing for the Cup.

She'd stayed out of trouble where Ethan was concerned. Even though she couldn't very well avoid him since she'd been tasked to assist him, she minimized private interactions and made sure others were around when she was with him to reduce temptation because tempted she was.

During the day she concentrated on team matters, but at night she succumbed to fantasies filled with sparkling blue eyes, a sexy half smile, and a hard, muscular body. Not that she'd seen him naked, but she could imagine. Thank God, the team's recent success had distracted her somewhat.

Lauren had pinched herself several times over the course of the last twenty-four hours as she realized how close this team was to achieving the impossible. They deserved this—every one of them, including the staff and coaches who'd worked so hard, slept little, and given it all to reach this point.

The team continued to play beyond their abilities, believing in themselves. And Cooper, who'd stuck with the team through all the adversity and losing seasons, had never once given up hope or sold out to the highest bidder. That type of loyalty didn't exist in pro sports anymore. Cooper said once in a rare interview that you could only spend so much money, and the extra dollars didn't come close to making up for the team and community relationships he'd built over the years.

And Cooper *had* built relationships. He worked tirelessly on his different causes, especially children's cancer, faithfully spending one day a week at the Children's Hospital. He'd rarely missed a week in all the years he'd been with the team.

Ethan needed to see that side of Cooper, understand where he was coming from, and appreciate him for the man he was off the ice as well as on the ice.

She'd finally done a few cursory searches on Ethan Williams

and Brad Reese. Zero information came up that she could identify as either men, which was actually a little odd in itself, almost as if they didn't exist. She tabled the sleuthing for now, grateful nothing surfaced to validate her worries. She dealt in facts, and so far none of the facts substantiated her intuition.

The team had a few days before the next series began, and Lauren suspected Coop would be heading to the hospital with some teammates. Playing the stalker, she hung out until he finished practice and ambushed him as he walked off the ice.

Usually happy to see her, Cooper pursed his lips, his eyes wary, as if her association with Ethan branded her as a possible traitor. Cooper didn't like change. He liked everything all lined up, neat and tidy. His insistence on structure served him well on the ice, where his precision counted big time. Off the ice, she wished the Giants' star player would be a little more flexible, more open-minded to the possibilities of life without the Sleezers.

"Are you going to see your kids this afternoon after practice?" she asked him.

He stiffened and lifted his chin, setting his jaw and regarding her with a hooded gaze, as if he were trying to decipher her ulterior motives. "Yeah, Ced and I are."

"Good. Mind if Ethan and I tag along?" Lauren clutched her hands behind her back to hide her fidgeting.

Cooper frowned. Oh, yeah, he minded, really minded, but he sighed, as if he knew arguing would get him nowhere. "If that's what you want."

"What time and where should we meet you?"

"We'll be at the hospital around two P.M. You can meet us there." He slipped past her as if he couldn't get away fast enough.

So much for traveling in the same car, but Lauren would take what she got. Cooper was the easy part. Now to convince Ethan and to keep the two men from killing each other.

* * * *

Ethan didn't see the point in invading Cooper's private time, but Lauren wouldn't back down. She wanted him to see a different side of Cooper. Feeling cranky and unsure why, Ethan tagged along.

Lauren pulled her piece-of-crap car into the visitor parking at the University of Florida hospital. He rubbed the back of his neck and stared out the passenger window, not convinced this was a good idea.

"I don't think Cooper will appreciate me being here."

"Hang with me on this." Lauren turned off the engine and got out, leaving him no choice but to follow or sit inside a car with the blistering sun beating down. He hurried to catch up, still annoyed for no good reason. She punched the button for the fourth floor.

"This is not a good idea." Ethan spoke quietly as they got off the elevator. At the end of the hall, a commotion caught his attention.

"Neither was you walking into the locker room after a game, but you did it anyway." Lauren's teasing smile thawed his irritation. She touched his arm, and the contact did weird shit to him, reminding him of the very reason he'd been trying his damnedest to avoid her. Impossible to do, but he'd given it a shot. She'd done the same, and for that, he'd been grateful. Nothing good would come of a physical relationship with her no matter how hard his dick wanted in the game.

She stopped near a set of open double doors and pointed inside, giddy with excitement. Ethan couldn't take his eyes off her. God, she was lovely when she lit up from the inside out. He swallowed hard and stepped closer on the pretense of looking inside the room. Hell, he didn't even glance at the scene in the room. His eyes locked onto hers like a targeting device and refused to move.

"Ethan?" She touched his arm, and he jerked himself to attention.

"Uh, yeah?"

She pointed again, her gaze darting from him to the room and back again. "It'll be good for you to see Cooper and the guys in action off the ice."

"Okay." Reluctantly, he looked away from her, but he still sensed her closeness, almost as if she were touching him even though she wasn't.

Beyond them was a large playroom full of kids dressed in hospital gowns and in various sizes and shapes, some in wheelchairs, a few running around as if nothing were physically wrong. Except for their predominantly bald heads, most of them could be kids anywhere.

Ethan stared at his star player, the guy with an attitude bigger than Mount Rainier and plenty of opinions. Cooper joked and played with the kids, his expression soft and gentle. Some of the little ones hung on him, others crowded around him. A few of the sicker ones eagerly waited with hope and patience which tugged at Ethan's heart. Other members of the team worked the room, but Cooper appeared to be the real star in this show and the ringleader of the group.

Something was missing.

Ethan glanced around the room, trying to figure it out. Then it came to him. No TV cameras. No reporters. This was strictly an off-the-record visit. These guys were here because they wanted to be, not for a promo op. That said a lot about their character. A sliver of pride vibrated through him. Maybe he didn't have the right to be proud of this team, but he was. He'd made the perfect choice in going after them, even if it'd take a while for them to appreciate him as much as he appreciated them.

"Do they do this often?" He lowered his voice, not wanting to call attention to himself.

"Every chance they get. They also visit veterans' homes and nursing homes."

Ethan nodded as he followed Lauren into the room. They sat in a corner at a small inconspicuous table.

"Cooper is a fixture in this city. He does tons of charity work, much of it anonymously, like working with these kids."

Ethan said nothing as he watched Coop entertain the dozen or so kids sitting around in wheelchairs and on the couches. He steeled himself against emotions he didn't want to feel. These kids idolized Cooper. They hung on his every word as he talked about enjoying every moment of life and being a good person.

This was going to be hard. Harder than Ethan had ever imagined. He'd always thought of this move from Seattle's point of view. He'd be the hero, the guy who gave Seattle back a winter sport since their beloved Sonics left. Now he was about to steal another city's team.

He rolled his shoulders, trying to ease some of the tension gripping his body. This was business, and sometimes the tough choices hurt innocent people.

In its current location, this hockey team hemorrhaged money. In Seattle, it stood an excellent shot at being a lucrative investment and a Seattle icon for years to come. Ethan's business dealings were all about making the hard choices. This project would be no different, except while he was making Seattle's dreams come true, he'd be ripping out the hearts of hockey fans in this area.

"What are you thinking?"

He snapped his head in Lauren's direction. "Why do you ask?"

"You seem disturbed when you should be anything but. Why, Ethan? What's bothering you?"

Her concern touched him. No one had worried about him since he'd been a little kid. What Ethan would give for a woman like Lauren with whom he could share all his troubles, wishes, and desires. Like his father shared everything with his mother.

When the truth was revealed, she'd never trust him again. If he was lucky, she'd at least tolerate him as her employer and not bolt out the door and his life.

Ethan, my man, he thought, *you're skating on thin ice in the middle of a deep lake while it cracks all around you, but the only thing you can do is keep skating for the other side because you've come too far to go back now.*

Chapter 9—Cross-Checking

The day after the hospital visit, the commissioner called Ethan to an impromptu meeting at a bar near the airport.

The second Ethan walked into the bar, he knew something was up. He took a seat, ordered a whiskey and waded through small talk, when all he wanted to do was scream, *get to the point.*

Finally Straus did, and it wasn't what Ethan wanted to hear. His jaw dropped as he stared at the man. "What do you mean the league has to consider other offers?"

"We've been approached by another interested party." The coward wouldn't even meet his gaze.

"I bought this team, and if it wasn't for your gag order, the entire world would know by now, and there'd be no going back." Ethan fisted his hands under the table so he wouldn't wrap them around Straus's neck.

"We want a presence in Seattle. It's a huge, untapped hockey market, but we have an offer that'll keep the team in this city." Straus's gaze darted around the room, as if he were seeking an escape route.

"Offer? You shouldn't be considering other offers. This team is sold for all intents and purposes. You know as well as I do that even with a playoff run, the Giants are hemorrhaging money. New ownership won't change the fact the city has other draws for people's entertainment dollars, and hockey isn't at the top of their list." Ethan was incredibly frustrated. This was supposed to be a done deal, blessed by the league to rectify an unfortunate situation, and put a team in a bigger market with a better TV deal.

"The offer comes from well-respected men in the world of hockey. I'm concerned about repercussions from other team owners once this gets out regarding our hasty decision to allow this sale."

"Because I'm not a hockey guy? And none of my partners are hockey guys?"

Straus stared at his hands. "No, that's not it."

Liar. "What's the offer?" Ethan forced out the words from between gritted teeth. He'd be damned if he'd lose this team now.

"I'm not at liberty to say."

"Whatever it is, I'm raising my offer by one hundred million over whatever they come up with." Ethan sat back and crossed his arms over his chest. *Take that, asshole. If money talks, then mine is shouting.*

"You don't know what their offer is." Straus finally met his gaze. He swiped at the thin layer of sweat beading his brow, even though it was freezing-butt cold in this bar.

"I don't give a shit. That's my offer. This is my team, and we had a deal. I'm holding you to it." Ethan raised his chin and leaned forward. Straus shrank back in his seat.

"I'll need to consult with the relocation committee."

"Consult with them all you want. As soon as this team finishes its last game, I'll be announcing my purchase and the move."

"You can't do that." The commissioner sat up straighter and met his gaze, as if attempting to intimidate. Ethan almost laughed as he glared right back, and the man quickly looked away.

"I can, and I will. I have it in writing. You do recall our contract?"

The commissioner nodded and scratched his arm, glancing toward the doorway.

"Is that all?" Ethan was fighting mad and needed to get the hell out of here before he lost it and said something that couldn't be taken back. Not waiting for a response, he stood and strode toward the door, leaving the bastard to pay the bill.

* * * *

Lauren glanced up as her father walked into her office and shut the door. "Hey, Dad, what's up?"

"I have it from a good source, Williams is at an afternoon meeting with the commissioner right now."

"I know he is. It's not like it's a deep, dark secret. He has a lot of meetings with Straus."

Her father muttered something about Ethan having his head stuck up Straus's ass. "I want you to find out what was discussed. My group made their official offer yesterday."

Lauren fought back an odd rush of panic. Her pulse raised and her stomach clenched, her loyalties completely divided. "He won't tell me anything, Dad. You know that."

"So study his body language, his mood; those things tell more than his words. I want to know everything, every little nuance."

"I'll do what I can." She mumbled, not committing to her father's cause, even if guilt pressured her to comply.

"Lauren, this is important. We want this team, the boys and I. You do want to keep your job, don't you?"

Lauren bristled at the veiled insult that the only way she could get and keep a job with a team was because of her father's influence. Sure, he'd helped following the Max debacle after she'd ran back to Florida with her tail between her legs, but now her track record should speak for itself.

Besides, she wanted the job indicated by her title, not a glorified clerical position in which the men in charge sent her to make copies—who used paper copies anymore anyway?—and discounted everything she said or even worse, patronized her. Her dad's good ol' boy group would never give her the credit or clout she'd worked so hard to earn. She didn't mind working twice as hard as any man, but eventually she wanted the respect she deserved and a shot at moving up based on her merits, not the size of her dick.

Ethan had given her respect from the very beginning. He depended on her input and asked her opinions, never once giving a shit she was female, while her very own father discounted her opinions on all things hockey. Yet, this wasn't all about Lauren. It was about winning, putting the best possible product on the ice, and giving the guys every chance to succeed. Deep down, the current coaching staff and management weren't getting it done. They'd been lucky and riding the backs of guys playing out of their hearts and minds. Ethan knew that as well as she did. Did anyone else get it?

"Dad, I want to keep this job, but I want more responsibility."

Her father scowled, reminding her of when she was little girl and she taxed him with one of her many questions about why the boys got to do things she didn't. "Lauren, honey, I know you were a good hockey player, you know hockey, but you can never know hockey at the level of someone who's played on a men's team and especially in the NHL. You're doing really well. Be happy with that."

"Because I don't have balls, I'm relegated to support roles, not decision-making ones."

"Now, Lauren."

God, she hated it when he tried to placate her. "Ethan would give me more responsibility."

Her father took a step back and shook his head in disbelief. "Lauren, I'm going to pretend I didn't hear that."

"But you did, Dad. You heard it. Just because I didn't play the game at the level you did, doesn't mean I can't see things that are wrong, or I can't make contributions."

Lon just smiled, one of those infuriatingly patronizing smiles. "I'm sure you can, honey." He glanced at his watch. "Gotta go. Late for a meeting."

He hurried away, just like he had every other time involving tough situations with his daughter. It wasn't that he didn't love her, but he'd spent his entire life surrounded my men, and he had no idea how to handle his daughter.

Lauren sighed and returned to her spreadsheets, evaluating the team's performance in the last round of the playoffs, while waiting anxiously for Ethan to return from his meeting. Finally, after six PM, he called and asked if she wanted to discuss the finals over dinner. He said he was famished.

Despite her promise to avoid private situations with him, she caved at the note of despair in his voice. He needed her, and very few people needed her. Not like that.

She waited for Ethan at the pizza joint down the road from the arena and found a seat in a high-backed booth.

The epiphany hit her with the speed of Cooper driving to the net. *She wanted Ethan to be involved with the Giants on a long-term basis.* In fact, she counted on it. Ethan's steady leadership would do more for this team than her father's good ol' boy group of hockey guys. Ethan with his passion for the game, his open-minded acceptance of new ways of training and coaching, and his respect for her and her knowledge.

She looked up from the menu she held in her hands as Ethan walked in. Lauren didn't have to be good at deciphering body language to notice the defeated slump of his shoulders, which went against the grain for what she knew about this man. He slipped into the booth and clutched the menu, not making eye contact.

"You look like you could use a friend," Lauren said.

He glanced over the top of his menu and smiled, though it didn't reach his eyes. "You're right about that." His wry smile said it all. Lauren wanted to wrap her arms around him and absorb his pain as hers, while he did the same for her.

"After this past month together, I could say we're friends."

He nodded, not disputing her statement, which gave her the courage to press on.

"How did the meeting with the big man go?" She spoke casually, as if his answer were of no consequence to her, yet in some ways it was everything.

"Not as planned, I'll say that much." Ethan leaned his elbows on the table and signaled for the waitress to order a bottle of wine.

"Does this have anything to do with another group trying to buy the team?"

His head shot up. His eyes narrowed in typical Ethan fashion. "You know about that?"

"My dad's involved." There, she'd said it, as simple as that, and laid it out on the table, that thing which had been between them for a few weeks.

"I didn't know whether or not he'd say anything to you since you're working closely with the enemy." Ethan eyed her carefully, as if discerning where she stood. How the hell could he know, when she wasn't even sure?

Lauren smiled. "You're not the enemy. Both groups want this team. No enemies here."

"No, just one winner and one loser." With that statement, he'd hit the puck in the net.

"I know." Lauren admitted.

He leaned forward, his chin propped in his hands. "Tell me, you've been with the team for years. What's your assessment of this market? Will it sustain this team on a long-term basis? I know the statistical answer to this question, but I want an honest, gut feeling from a fan and employee whose heart bleeds for this organization and believes in it one-hundred percent."

Lauren hesitated, her first inclination to defend the city and the fans, but honesty and common sense won over loyalty. "I don't think so, even with the Sleezers out of it." She spoke quietly, almost a whisper.

"Your dad's group. Will they be able to afford to keep this team in town on a permanent basis? Do they have that kind of big money backing them? The Giants have been partially financed by the league for quite a while."

"The better question would be—can your group afford to keep

the team here with possible years of financial loss and no plan for a new arena?" She shot the question back to him.

"Can any ownership group if they're good businessmen?" His face revealed nothing.

"Probably not." Her heart dived as she said the dreaded words, knowing any infusion of money into this team only put a Band-Aid on a gaping wound.

"So we're looking at the possibility any future ownership would eventually be forced to move the team regardless of their intentions?" His Caribbean blue eyes met and held hers, as if he needed her as a sounding board. "I can't guarantee my ownership group will keep this team in Florida."

"Is there something you're not telling me, Ethan?" She pried her gaze away from his and once again flipped through the menu.

"What's your assessment of your dad's ownership group?" He slyly avoided the question.

She hesitated, but her instincts aligned her with Ethan, as stupid and dangerous as that might be. "They're great old-school hockey guys."

"But? I hear a but..."

She didn't answer.

"Lauren, I need to know what you think." He snatched the menu from her and grabbed both of her hands, holding them tightly as he leaned forward, his gaze intent on her face. "Tell me, please."

Lauren stared at her hands in his larger ones and cleared her throat. "This team isn't going to win it all with old-school hockey. We don't have the traditional player types needed to do so. We'll have to employ more inventive means, more mixing up the lines, choosing and keeping players with valuable skills you can't measure with normal statistics. Last year we let a young guy go because he didn't have the big-time stats, but he did things to get the puck in the right place, stuff my statistical analysis measured, but their old school stuff did not. His absence hurt us this year, big time."

"I bet you wanted them to keep him?"

Lauren nodded. "But they wouldn't listen."

"They don't listen to you much, do they?"

Suddenly, Lauren choked up, and she hated it. She shook her head, unable to speak without blubbering. Silently she cursed this female weakness, which reared its ugly head at the most inopportune times.

"Lauren." His voice turned gentle and her body turned to jelly. He slipped out of his side of the booth and slid in next to her, put his arm around her, and tucked her to his side. His comfort felt as natural as breathing. She clung to him, burying her face in his shoulder, even as her body was racked with sobs of frustration she'd held in check for too long. He wrapped her in his strong, calm presence, almost making her believe he could keep the wolves at bay from sheer force of will.

Max used to make her feel like that in the early days, like she was the most important thing on earth and together they could do anything. She'd fallen for his attentiveness and consideration as if she mattered, because she'd never mattered before, except maybe to Aunt Jo. But Max's caring gestures had been an illusion carefully crafted to keep her clueless. And clueless she'd been until checks started bouncing, bills piled up, and her once-loving husband choose puck bunnies and booze over her.

And she trusted Ethan why? It wasn't like she was a good judge of character or anything. Max had ripped her heart out, and now she'd turned down that road again, unable to stop herself.

Ethan stroked her hair, and she wanted to fall back into denial. "It's okay, honey. It is. I know it's tough but don't give up. Don't let them win. I understand what it's like to be discounted and treated like you don't know shit."

Something he said struck a chord in her; hell, it played the entire piano. Wiping her eyes, she looked up at him. "I did that to you, didn't I? I kept telling you that you weren't a hockey guy. I blew off your opinions just like they do to me."

"It's all right." He smiled and shrugged, not holding it against her.

"I'm sorry. I didn't—I didn't realize I'd done to you what they do to me."

"Even your dad?"

"Especially my dad. He barely knows I exist. I have two brothers in the NHL, one older, one younger."

"I know." His mouth twitched in a smile.

"Of course, you know. He'll call them and discuss a player even though they're on competing teams before he'll consider talking to me."

Ethan frowned and for a moment his eyes got hard, but they softened just as quickly, and he sighed. "I'm sure my sister would say that our dad doesn't consider her opinions as strongly as he does his sons'. He's not a bad person, and he tries, but it's hard when you've been raised in a culture that values men in business or in sports."

Lauren rubbed her eyes, grateful she never wore enough makeup to smudge it. "I cut him some slack because he does try. Sometimes. He means well."

"We're all doing the best we can with the knowledge and limitations we have at the time, Lauren. Just remember that." His words sounded ominous.

She nodded and sniffed. He kept his arm around her, and she didn't pull away. She liked it too much, liked the feel of his warm, hard body next to hers, liked the scent of that spicy aftershave, and wanted this man in ways she'd never imagined, doing things she'd never imagined with anyone else. Not even Max.

They ate dinner and made small talk, drinking a bottle of wine in the process.

"So Ethan, I've been honest with you. Now it's your turn." Lauren pushed her plate away, ready to ask the tough questions.

He visibly stiffened, his smile brittle and his gaze wary. "Okay."

"Do you have a future with this team or are you gone once your job here is done?"

He didn't answer at first. Instead he swirled the wine around in his glass as if it were more fascinating than the third period of game seven of the Cup with a tied score. "Yeah, I have a place if I want it."

"Do you? Want it, that is?" She watched him closely, looking for something, though not sure what, but she'd know when she found it.

"Yes. I'll be in a management role." He turned to her, his eyes glinting with determination. "I want you there with me, Lauren."

She pointed at herself, humbled, honored, and a little taken aback. "You do?"

"I do. I want you doing what you're good at, evaluating each player's strengths and weaknesses. Figuring out how to maximize their strengths. Running those incredible stats of yours and analyzing them to give our GM an advantage over other organizations."

"Ike would never go for that stuff. He thinks it's bullshit."

When Ethan didn't answer, the cold hand of dread wrapped its bony fingers around her heart and squeezed.

"Is Ike being fired, Ethan?"

"No one's going to be fired. They'll all get a fair shot. I promise you."

"Even my dad who's been lobbying for different ownership?" How ironic would that be to have a job over her father? The thought gave her no satisfaction.

He nodded. "Even your dad. He doesn't know my potential ownership group so why should he feel loyal and why would I hold that against him?"

"You have a point. You're a fair man, Ethan Williams."

Instead of being flattered, he cringed. "I try to be when the situation allows it."

Lauren tilted her head and eyed him, not sure what his statement meant exactly. "I think it's time I should be going."

"I didn't see your car out there."

"I walked to work this morning and then walked here from the arena."

Ethan stood and held out a hand. "Let me give you a lift home. This isn't the best of neighborhoods, and it'll be dark in an hour or so."

Lauren nodded, not even attempting to win his argument and secretly not wanting to win it. She was tired of fighting this attraction, tired of denying their mutual chemistry, just damn tired of not getting what she really wanted.

And she wanted Ethan in the worst possible way.

Just like she'd wanted Max.

* * * *

Ethan put the key in the ignition and drove Lauren home to a modest apartment building. It appeared well-maintained with four units on each of two floors, in a decent neighborhood surrounded by tidy little single-family homes.

He'd been as honest as he'd dared with her, considering his now-precarious position with the commissioner and the league. Telling her everything sat on the tip of his tongue, but he bit it back.

He'd as good as told he'd be in team management and the team would be moving, he just hadn't told her how soon.

Volunteering to take her home after the day they'd both had probably wasn't at the top of his bright-idea list, but he'd never been one to pay attention to lists or rules, and he wasn't now.

Lauren turned in the seat to face him, her beautiful eyes more brown than green, which seemed to happen when she was concerned. "Ethan, you never told me what happened with the commissioner and why you looked like your mama ran off with a twenty-something pool boy."

Ethan chuckled. "Trust me, my mother would never do that."

"All the more devastating if it happened since you seem to think it wouldn't."

"Lauren, I truly appreciate your concern, but I have to work this out myself." He grabbed her hands and held them, something he'd done way too much tonight, but he loved the feeling of her soft hands in his. Ethan leaned closer, and she did too, neither of them saying a word, because words might slap some sense into them.

God, he was going to regret this, and he'd chastise himself for once again being too weak to resist, but damn it all to hell, he was tired of telling himself no, not when she looked at him with intense hazel eyes, now this incredible green which reminded him of the sun filtering through the trees in a forest.

"Lauren," he rasped as he framed her expressive face in his hands and drowned in those incredible eyes.

"Ethan," she whispered in response.

Oh, shit, she wasn't going to stop him. His erection pushed against his fly, warning it sure as hell wouldn't be stopping him. And his head appeared to have ordered takeout, while it settled in for the show. No help there either.

He brushed his lips against hers, tasting, and circling back to taste more deeply. She melted against him, despite the console separating their lower bodies—good thing, really.

He explored, pillaged, plundered, and savored at the same time, feasting like a starving man on all she offered. Her moans of pleasure against his mouth wiped out what little brain function remained, and his primal instincts kicked in. He buried his fingers in her hair and pulled her closer across the console.

She felt like all of life's great memories rolled into one

incredible kiss. She tasted even better, and he couldn't get enough. Neither could she. Her tongue danced with his, as she wrapped her arms around his neck, panting, squirming, and begging for more.

Damn, but he wanted to give her more. He wanted to give her everything. Ethan slid his hand under her blouse, and she trembled as his warm palm contacted her bare skin. His hands shook slightly. He dragged his mouth from hers and kissed his way across her cheek.

"You are so incredible," he whispered against her cheek. "So incredible."

"So are you." Her breathless voice slipped past his carefully constructed defenses, leaving him dazed by the sheer power of the emotions careening inside him.

"Sweetheart, you taste and feel like nothing I've ever imagined."

She nipped at his earlobe and moaned as he rubbed his thumb across one nipple through the fabric of her bra.

"You're making it hard for me to behave," she said.

"Then don't." He pushed her shirt upward, needing to see more of her.

A motorcycle started up very close by and drowned out the sounds of their heavy panting and murmured words of encouragement.

"Damn." Ethan muttered as he glanced around for the location of the bike, a Harley by the sounds of it.

"Damn." Lauren scrambled over the console to the passenger seat and smoothed her hair, regarding Ethan with wary, ashamed eyes.

Ethan was the one who should be ashamed, especially considering the position of power he held over her, or would in the near future. Yet he couldn't bring himself to apologize. He'd lied so many times. He couldn't lie about this. He wasn't sorry. Not one damn bit, and he'd do it again in a heartbeat. The only thing he felt sorry about was her obvious regret.

"I need to go in. We fly out in the morning. It's a big day for the team." Lauren opened the door and bolted for her apartment. Ethan leapt out and caught up with her in several long strides.

He grabbed her hand before she could escape. "Don't regret what happened, Lauren. Please, don't regret it."

94

"It was a mistake." She stared up at him through lowered lashes.

"A mistake between two people who have an undeniable attraction to each other. I don't see that as a mistake." Who was he kidding? Of course, it was a mistake, and she didn't know the entire story. The truth of it hit him squarely between the eyes—he'd do it again given half the chance.

She stared him directly in the eyes. "I do."

He framed her face in his hands. "Well, you shouldn't. Nothing that feels this good could ever be a mistake." Ethan dipped his head and took her mouth once again, her plump lips already swollen from his earlier kisses. She stiffened, and he half-expected her to jerk away, but she didn't. Instead her arms twined around his neck, and she leaned into him, her body pressed against his length. He cupped her sweet ass in his hands and lifted her upward, dragging her crotch across his dick. He groaned at the torture of it all, cursing the clothes separating them, and knowing if those clothes didn't exist, he'd lift her butt onto the porch railing and plunge deep into the greatest heaven known to man, especially this man with this woman.

Clothes be damned, he sat her fine ass on the rail and humped her with all the finesse of a dog on the prowl. Her skirt hiked up her thighs, and she wrapped her mostly bare legs around his waist and ground her crotch into his. Her whimpers sent him over the edge and his kisses roughened, demanding and promising at the same time. Her mouth spoke of undeniable lust, explosive chemistry, and ragged desire without uttering a word.

He slid his hands up her blouse and cupped her rounded breasts, not too large, not too small, just perfect. Her nipples hardened through her lacy bra. Dragging his mouth from her lips, he rained little kisses down her neck and nibbled on her collarbone.

"I want to get naked with you, Lauren."

"Just get naked. That's it?"

"Oh, no, that's the appetizer. I want the whole five-course meal."

She leaned away from him, blinking a few times then smiled. "I bet you say that to all the women."

"I bet I don't."

Lauren wrapped her fingers around his collar and stared up at him. She chewed on her lower lip, looking as if she were considering his proposition. Finally she rested her forehead on his chest and heaved a deep sigh. Ethan heaved one of his own. He knew her answer.

Stepping away, Lauren fumbled to turn her key in the lock. Once the door was open, she turned to him. "Good night, Ethan."

"Good night, Lauren," he said as the door shut in his face. He stared at it for a long time, willing her to come back outside and invite him in. She didn't. Instead the outside light flicked off and cloaked him in darkness.

With a frustrated groan, he trudged back to the car. Bad idea to try to sleep with her, to even tell her that he wanted her, but he just wanted to have her once so he could carry the memory of that moment with him for the rest of his life.

He had a week at the least and a month and a half at the most before the news got out, assuming the deal didn't fall through. This was about business, about the goal within his reach, not about messing with a staff person and in turn screwing this up.

Instead of muddying the waters with sex, he needed to determine if Lauren's loyalty to the team was stronger than her loyalty to her father. He wanted her tied up as an employee for his team, even though he'd love to tie her up in other ways, too.

Get your mind out of the gutter, Parker. This is about the game. The mission. The ultimate goal. Not about you getting your rocks off with a woman about to be your employee.

He could get physical relief elsewhere, but he couldn't duplicate Lauren's knowledge, drive, and dedication to the team and the game. That type of passion didn't skate across the ice every day. She was a big part of his future plans, as much as blue-chip players like Coop and Cedric.

He needed to win her over so when his true intentions came to light, she'd forgive him.

Winning her over did not include getting her naked.

Chapter 10—Cooper on Ice

Frustrated and angry with the league and his weakness toward Lauren, Ethan barely slept. Finally, at the crack of dawn, he gave up on sleep, packed a small suitcase for the two-day road trip, grabbed his skates, and headed to the rink. He had a few hours before the team buses loaded and left for the airport, and he'd been too long off the ice.

He needed a clear head and skating into exhaustion had a way of doing that.

Right now his thoughts bounced from the conversation with the commissioner to his conflicting feelings about Lauren, but his focus must stay on his mission.

To make the Seattle Sockeyes a reality at all costs.

Had the league played him for a fool? Used him to drive up the price of the team, only to back out and sell to an ownership group with intentions to keep the team in this city? All the long-term financial and attendance records proved that hockey didn't work here, and nothing could change that fact. Even if the league sold to the other group, the team would eventually move. The old arena was barely adequate, the facilities in disrepair, and the political climate didn't lend itself to public funds or support for a new rink.

Even more frustrating was the gag order. Ethan wanted to tell Lauren, pour out his heart, reveal his dream of bringing hockey to Seattle, and invite her on this journey with him. He wanted her to feel his passion for the city and the market, to understand he didn't want to hurt anyone, but the situation forced one city to be the loser, and it damn well wouldn't be Seattle.

With a heavy sigh, Ethan laced his skates and stepped onto the ice, leaving his doubts and fears in the bleachers. Only a few lights were on in the rink. He'd snuck in long before the coaching staff and team showed up to skate laps. He loved the sound of his blades cutting into the ice as he leaned into his turns. Loved the way his blood pumped through his veins as he raced down the long side. Skating had always been an outlet for his emotions, that place he went to escape the outside world. It was just him, the ice, and his blades.

He took a few leisurely turns around the rink to warm up before he felt eyes on him and realized he wasn't alone. He glanced over his shoulder to see Cooper step onto the ice and glide toward him with long easy strides until they were side by side. Ethan continued to skate as if they did this every morning.

"Didn't realize you skated." Cooper's voice held a neutrality not usually reserved for Ethan.

Ethan skated several more feet before answering. "There's a lot of things you don't know about me. I'm surprised you're here this early." Ethan pushed aside a rare moment of insecurity as Cooper fell silent. He could feel the man's eyes on him, evaluating for weaknesses, no doubt.

"Seriously? I want to get in a skate before we fly out. I'm surprised *you're* here."

"I needed time on the ice. It relaxes me."

"I know that story."

Cooper kicked it up a notch, and Ethan's competitive drive pushed him to skate harder. As futile as it was to skate with one of the fastest skaters in professional hockey, Ethan couldn't stop himself. They sped around the corners, Ethan breathing hard, Cooper barely breaking a sweat. The man could sprint away and leave Ethan in the dust at any moment, but oddly enough, he didn't.

"You have a pretty good rhythm going there, but you're leaning too far forward. Keep your body straighter, and push out to the side, not straight back."

Ethan didn't dare expend excess energy by answering—he needed everything he had to concentrate on his skating technique and breathing. It wasn't often a fan got a lesson from one of the all-time greats. Cooper pushed him harder, faster, as they raced around the rink. He seemed to know just how hard to push Ethan without completely destroying him.

Ethan held his own and when they finally slowed, he saw the grudging respect in Cooper's eyes. They cooled down in silence except for the swoosh of their skates on ice. Finally Ethan slid to a stop. Cooper did, too.

"Not bad for an amateur. How long have you been skating?"

"Since college, before that just a little bit here and there."

"If you'd started as a kid, you might've had a chance making hockey a career. You're athletic." Cooper paid Ethan a rare compliment.

"I played football."

Cooper shrugged. "Nothing wrong with that. I never had time for it. Hockey consumed me. It's been my life since I put on my first set of skates."

"Most NHL players are like that," Ethan conceded. "More than other athletes, it seems."

"Hockey is a three-hundred-sixty-five-day-a-year commitment."

Ethan nodded. A hockey player's commitment to his sport was one of the things which attracted Ethan to owning a hockey team.

"How long have you been skating here in the mornings?"

"This is the first time, but I skate at home every day. Keeps me in shape, and I enjoy it more than running."

Cooper studied him for a long moment. "I'll meet you for a skate same time tomorrow morning."

"We're in Boston tomorrow."

"Yeah, so?"

"Sounds good." Ethan kept it light, like it wasn't a big deal one way or another. But it was—a really big deal.

Without another word, Cooper returned to his skating drills. Ethan hesitated and decided to get out of there before anyone else caught him. He'd attempted to keep his skating private, but he'd skate for national TV if it allowed him to bond with his star player. He had a foot in the door with Cooper; now if he could just win the guy over before the word got out Ethan was a big, fat fraud.

After Lauren, Cooper would be the first person he'd talk to once the gag order was lifted. He owed him that. Hopefully, he could do a strong enough sell job his star would cooperate. The rest of the team would follow Cooper anywhere.

Ethan just hoped *anywhere* was in the Pacific Northwest.

* * * *

One night later, Lauren sat with Ethan on the glass amidst a fervent Boston crowd. She glanced around warily, not liking the charged atmosphere when her boys weren't playing at home. Hopefully, they'd feed off the noise even if it wasn't for them.

She tugged on her skirt and smoothed the wrinkles out of it, glad she'd gone for prim and proper instead of team loyalty. Loyalty didn't mean shit when an angry or celebratory crowd mobbed her for wearing the opposing team's colors.

"Are you sure we're safe sitting down here?" Lauren glanced over her shoulder at the two drunken idiots behind them as she gripped her tablet tightly. Gritting her teeth she faced forward and gazed around the sea of green and white.

Ethan nodded. "We're not wearing Giants jerseys, so we should be fine."

"Why do you like to sit down here? The view is better up there." She pointed to the suites.

He raised one dark brow. God, even his eyebrows were sexy. "The Sleezers are up there." He slanted one of those boyish, sexy smiles at her, the kind that made her mentally fan herself and wish she could turn her internal AC on high.

Lauren laughed in spite of her nervousness. "You have a point."

"A really big point. Can't stand those pricks."

"On that subject we totally agree."

His expression softened, sending her heart into arrhythmia. "We agree on a lot of things, Lauren."

She locked eyes with his and like every other time, he seemed to read her every thought. She looked away, pretending to consult notes on her tablet. He said nothing. When she looked up again, he was staring at the ice, watching the players go through passing and scoring drills.

"We shouldn't even be here." Lauren shook her head in amazement.

"We shouldn't? Don't worry, I'll protect you, honey." He winked at her.

She glared at him. "The *team*. They shouldn't be here according to all the predictions and analysis." The Giants had been ranked at the bottom of the division at the beginning of the season. They barely made the playoffs, and now they were seven games away from skating for the Cup.

Incredible. And a real testament to the men down there on the ice, who'd played like a team with a destiny greater than the sum of their parts. There weren't any show-boaters. Every one of them contributed unselfishly as part of a team. She'd like to give the coaches credit for fine-tuning the Giants into a well-honed machine, but she knew better. Cooper and the other captains ran the show.

"Lauren," Ethan said, drawing her attention back to him. "There's one thing you can't analyze, and that's *try*. These guys have it in spades. I'd choose a team with average talent and exceptional drive over an exceptionally talented team with average drive any day of the season and especially when it's for the Cup. Then all bets are off."

"We're still a few guys away from building a team around Cooper and Cedric that could be a contender season after season."

"That's my assessment, too." Ethan turned in his seat, his expression earnest. "I've been talking to the ownership group about you. They want you, and they're willing to pay you a generous salary if you'll commit to the team for a year."

Lauren swallowed and stared at the ice. This was what she'd wanted, what she'd worked for, not the money, but the respect, the opportunity to use her knowledge to contribute to the construction of a perennial winner rather than contribute to the copier count or a full pot of coffee. Ethan was handing her dream job to her in a silver cup as big as the Stanley.

But there was the matter of her father and her obligation to him. Not to mention the man knew how to hold a grudge, and even as his daughter, she never wanted to be on the receiving end of his retribution.

"Can we talk about it later?" she said as the puck dropped and the crowd whipped itself into a frenzy, ruling out any further discussion.

Ethan grinned at her and turned back to the game. Lauren did so too, though her mind went somewhere else and that somewhere had to do with the sexy businessman sitting in the next seat and his offer.

* * * *

After the game, a close three-to-four loss, Ethan headed for the hotel bar with Lauren in tow. Not a player in sight, partially because of curfew and partially exhaustion. After a private team dinner in a banquet room, Coop and Cedric had herded them off to bed.

Ethan and Lauren ate dinner and discussed the loss, evaluating everything in minute detail. Ethan prolonged the inevitable goodnights, not wanting to part from Lauren. He craved everything about her, from her open, genuine smile to her ability to put him in his place with one withering look, to her conservative business suits. His mother would adore her except that Lauren worked for him or would soon. That wouldn't go over well, especially after his one disastrous work relationship. Several million dollars and burning embarrassment later, he'd been screwed so badly, he'd avoided anything beyond one-night stands. So why was he thinking about another personal relationship with a co-worker?

Lauren.

Her name conjured up an image of another Lauren, along with old black and white movies back in the days when romance was romantic. Ethan wasn't much for romance, but with the right woman he might be swayed to find a romantic bone in his body, while he was finding all those things he loved about her body.

Shit.

He ran his hand through his too-long hair and scratched his chin, hating the scruff, but realizing the necessity.

"Was someone in your family a fan of Bogie and Bacall?" He asked conversationally because the topic skated on thicker ice than the one he really wanted to discuss.

She smiled up at him. "Yes, my great grandmother on my dad's side. She insisted I be named after Lauren Bacall. She thought I had those cat-like eyes even as a baby."

Ethan leaned forward and studied her. "You do have her eyes."

"Are you a fan?" She ducked her head, blushing.

He liked it when she blushed.

"Of you or her?" He chuckled and her eyes widened with shock. "The answer to both is yes."

"Ethan. We're colleagues, nothing else." Her face flushed an even darker shade of red, and he had to grin, feeling devilish for jerking her chain and enjoying every moment of it.

"We're more than that. We're friends, Lauren."

She didn't respond right away. "We are friends."

"Took you a while to figure that out."

"I have trust issues," she quipped.

He laughed, but inside his gut clenched. "Don't we all, Lauren? Don't we all?" He glanced at his phone. "We probably should call it a night. The staff is staring at us."

Lauren glanced around, surprised darkening those beautiful eyes of hers. "We're the only ones in here."

"That we are." Ethan paid the bill and stood, resting his hand on Lauren's back as he escorted her through the eerily quiet lobby and to the elevator. She punched her floor, and he punched his. They stood on opposite sides of the elevator, suddenly as uncomfortable as strangers.

Ethan felt the pull between them, an invisible cord tightening, attempting to bring them together. He took a step closer. So did she. Before he knew it, only a foot separated them. He put his hands on her shoulders and gently walked her backward until he'd pinned her against the elevator wall. Her lips parted, and he accepted the invitation.

The elevator dinged and the doors slid open. Brad walked in, and they jumped apart.

"What's up, kids?"

"You have the worst timing," Ethan growled.

"Looks like damn good timing to me." Brad grinned from ear to ear.

Ethan didn't feel like grinning. Not one damn bit. He felt like giving Brad's dentist some business by rearranging some of his teeth.

Lauren took advantage of the opportunity and slipped around them, down the hall, and into her room.

Ethan stared after her, pissed and relieved at the same time.

Chapter 11—Goal on Net

The Giants lost the first two semifinal games with Boston by one goal each, despite the brilliant play of Cooper and Cedric. The rest of the team played tired, and nothing Coop or Ced tried fired them up. Lauren bit off her fingernails in the process, and she hated jagged fingernails. After the elevator encounter, which she so *fondly* called it, she kept Ethan at arms' length, hard to do when circumstances forced them together at every turn.

Today was game three at home, and she couldn't sleep for a multitude of reasons. Finally, she gave up and headed to the arena to get an early start on her day and rid herself of disturbingly sexy dreams about one Ethan Williams.

Ethan's car was parked in the private lot behind the arena, along with Cooper's. Not unusual for either workaholic. Lauren searched the office areas, but couldn't find Ethan anywhere.

Worried he might have gotten into an altercation with Coop, she looked in the locker room, coach's office, players' lounge, and press corps area. Even the men's bathrooms. Nothing. Unless he was in the stands somewhere watching Coop skate his early morning workout. She walked onto the second level for a view of the lower level seats and the ice, almost dreading what she might find. Hopefully, not bloodshed.

Two men raced around the rink in the dimly lit arena. Their skates swooshed and sprayed ice as they leaned into the corners at breakneck speed.

Lauren did a double take and squinted. A triple take. She sat down hard on the nearest seat. And stared again. Shaking her head, she rubbed her eyes. Maybe she had a touch of the flu along with hallucinations. She felt her forehead, cool to the touch. How about a temporary bout of insanity? An alien abduction? None of those options seemed as farfetched as the two men flying around the arena as if they were best buddies in a friendly little competition. Ethan held his own, though she suspected—actually was certain—Coop wasn't putting out more than fifty percent as he pushed Ethan to skate harder. Judging by the sweat running off Ethan's brow and the lack of sweat on Coop's, Coop was doing a good job staying cool while Ethan bordered on passing out.

They circled a few more times, picked up their sticks, and

engaged in a game of man-on-man. Coop didn't hold back this time. He gave Ethan an exhibition he'd never forget, stealing the puck, hitting the net from any and all angles and distances. Sweaty and breathing hard, they finally cooled down and skated off the ice to the locker room. Their laughter echoed throughout the empty building long after the door shut behind them, and the sound shocked the hell out of Lauren.

How long had this been going on right under her nose? Why hadn't Ethan mentioned he was a decent hockey player? Not pro caliber but damn good for an amateur. Her father had been right all along; nothing was as it seemed.

She rubbed her eyes, still coming to terms with this discovery. Finally, she stood and walked down the stairs to the locker room and waited for Ethan to walk out. He emerged finally, smiling, with his dark hair wet from a recent shower, and his face flushed from the workout. He wore his usual wrinkled T-shirt and faded jeans. His blue eyes widened when he saw her, but he recovered quickly.

"Lauren. You're a little early this morning." His calm, deep voice gave away nothing.

"I had to get an early start. I have this slave-driving bastard the league requires I cater to, and he's demanding." The second the words escaped her mouth, Lauren slapped her hand over her mouth. "I shouldn't have said that. I—"

He quirked an eyebrow and smiled at her, one of those smiles she lived for. Then he nodded. "Let's get to work then. We wouldn't want to piss off the bastard."

Lauren agreed and minutes later they worked side by side. On the surface, a casual observer would never know about the sexual current arcing between them, but Lauren knew, and she knew Ethan did, too. He touched her too much for it to be an accident. It was a glorious, torturous day, and Lauren didn't want to be anywhere else in the world. She wondered if Ethan did.

Lauren kept her mouth shut about Ethan's skate with Cooper for the majority of the day until they were sitting in the empty stands watching the team warm up prior to the night's playoff game. Coop skated as if he'd had a week's rest instead of going like a crazy man this morning and during the last game two nights ago.

Lauren glanced at Ethan to find him watching her. His hungry expression almost sent her into cardiac arrest, but she wrestled her wild heart under a semblance of control. "You're full of surprises, Ethan Williams."

His gentle smile warmed her heart. "More than you know, Lauren." Something flickered in his blue eyes, almost like regret, which she didn't exactly understand.

"You and Coop? Who'd have thought you'd become best buddies?"

"I wouldn't go that far, but we've developed a healthy respect for each other." If her comment surprised him, he didn't show it.

"I saw you this morning. I didn't know you could skate."

The smile dropped off his face, but he recovered quickly and responded smoothly. "Not bad considering I'm not a hockey guy." Ethan jerked her chain, but she didn't mind. In fact, she liked it, in a weird way. She liked Ethan, despite her best efforts, and looked forward to a future working with him to make the Giants a team to be reckoned with year after year, which meant she was going to accept his proposal.

If she wanted a future with this team, they had to keep their relationship strictly business, which was getting more and more difficult day after day. The man cast hot looks in her direction whenever he thought she wasn't looking. He probably caught the same hot looks from her. In the elevator a few nights ago, she'd caught more than that, but Brad and fate intervened to stop the inevitable.

Was sleeping with Ethan inevitable? She feared it might be.

"You never told me you played hockey." Hurt and accusation crept into her voice despite her best efforts.

"What makes you think I do?" He cocked his head at her, and his lips tipped up in a cocky smirk.

"I watched you. You're not a pro, obviously—"

"Obviously," he repeated with a wry grin.

"But you played like a good amateur. There's no shame in that. You're athletic."

He shrugged. "I don't advertise that I play. I'm not that good. Didn't play much until college, but I got hooked on it because I had a Canadian uncle who was rabid about it. He'd played in the minors at one point in time and did some local broadcasting. Growing up, I spent a couple weeks in Vancouver every year with him. He'd take me skating every day, took me to Canucks games. I couldn't beat 'em."

"So you joined him?"

"Yeah, I played on a low-level intramural team at U-Dub. Now I play in an adult hockey league."

Lauren frowned at him. "U-Dub?"

Ethan's face paled, but he recovered quickly. "Yeah." He didn't elaborate. Not one bit.

Lauren wanted to push him for an explanation, but his reluctance held her back. She'd Google it later. "So you were serious about having a passion for the game?"

"You doubt me?"

Lauren had to smile. "The truth?"

"Nothing but." He put his hand over his heart and faked a serious expression.

"I did doubt you at first. You're an enigma."

Ethan shrugged and looked away from her. "Not really. Just a private man."

"And you don't let too many people in."

"Neither do you, Lauren, so we're a pair, aren't we?" He looked up, his blue eyes earnest. "If people think you're a novice, they drop clues they don't think you'll get. I'm here to evaluate the team, so it was best to keep my limited hockey knowledge a secret."

"Is that how you felt about me?" Lauren cleared her throat, which suddenly seemed dry, and fiddled with her tablet.

He nodded slowly and swallowed. "Yeah, somewhat. This is business, and I take it seriously."

Lauren looked back at her computer screen. "On that note, we have work to do."

Ethan looked almost sad. "Yes, we do."

* * * *

The Giants lost the next game, but came back like gangbusters in game four. Cooper's hat trick led the Giants to a 5-2 victory. The guys weren't finished yet, but they were down three to one. The team would be heading back to Boston for game five in front of that deafening crowd.

One thing became crystal clear to Ethan. This playoff run could end in one game, and he had to wrap Lauren up, professionally that was. Not that he wouldn't mind wrapping her up physically and emotionally, but he needed to stay focused on the goal, his mission. His dream hovered within his grasp—bringing professional hockey to Seattle.

Which brought his addled brain back to the most pressing subject of all. He couldn't afford to lose Lauren as an employee, and he was prepared to pay her a handsome salary along with a bonus. If he could wrap her up for a year or so, she'd have time to adjust to Seattle, forgive his deception, and get on board with the program. At least he hoped like hell a year would be enough.

The team flew to Boston the day before the game, and Ethan and Lauren flew with them. Time to put his plan into action. If the team lost tomorrow, it'd be too late. He had twenty-four hours. Ethan invited her to dinner to talk hockey. After dinner he sat back and sipped on a glass of wine, regarding Lauren with a forced smile on his face. Inside he was nervous as hell, feeling like a thirteen-year-old boy asking the prettiest girl in school to his first dance.

"I have a serious offer for you." He gulped down his wine and ordered another. Tonight he'd need all the help he could get, liquid or otherwise.

Her eyes filled with wariness as if she suspected his offer might be sexual in nature. Damn, he wished it could be. Ethan opened his briefcase, forcing his thoughts to focus strictly on business. He pulled out the employment contract Cyrus had sent yesterday, knowing he was doing a devious, sneaky thing but doing it anyway. He needed Lauren. Absolutely needed her in more ways than he cared to analyze.

"Read this." He pushed the contract across the table to her and gave her time to read it. Her eyes grew big, most likely spotting the dollar amount. In typical Lauren fashion, she took her time. Ethan forced himself not to fidget and wiped his sweaty palms on the napkin in his lap.

After an agonizing eternity, she stared up at him, speechless and shaking her head, as if words failed her.

Ethan rushed to explain before she turned him down. "Lauren, as I alluded to previously, the ownership group is prepared to make you a very handsome offer if you'll sign this employment contract."

"Handsome offer? This is an insane amount of money." Lauren stared hard at the contract, as if she couldn't quite believe what she was reading.

"You're worth every penny of it." He spoke with absolute sincerity. She was to him.

"They don't own the team yet. Why would they want to hire me?"

"They're willing to take the gamble. At the very least, you'll be paid a guaranteed amount for a year and a bonus for signing on regardless of this team's future. Besides, they do own a minor league team, so you'd have a job there if this deal fell through." He resisted the urge to cross himself, even though he wasn't Catholic. "Think about it. Same position, twice the money. But with a progressive management team committed to creating a winning culture extending beyond a few seasons."

"I don't know." She hedged.

Ethan tamped down the urge to plead. This was not the time for emotions but cold, hard logic and facts Lauren would appreciate. "If you stay, and your father's group buys the team, do you really think you'll get a similar offer? Or will they keep you in a clerical role with a fancy title?"

"Like I have now," she spoke softly.

"Yeah, like you have now. We're willing to give you a say in how this team is built and operates because we believe in you."

"We?" She studied him, but he didn't even blink.

He'd made a mistake saying "we," but he went with it. "Yes, we."

"Are you truly a part of the team's future?"

Ethan didn't miss a beat. "That's being negotiated." Not a total lie. He was still negotiating in his mind how big of a role he'd play with his team.

Lauren read through the contract again then looked up. "What is PSHA?"

"The initials of the ownership group."

"Why are you pushing this right now?" Her eyes narrowed, and he feared she was on to him.

"Because once the team is done for the season, things will happen fast."

Her skeptical look said it all, but she didn't turn him down. "One year is a long time to enter into an agreement with an anonymous organization."

"Six months, then. And you keep the money regardless of whether or not you stay with us."

She worked her jaw. He could tell the money tempted her, but he doubted for a second that money was what drove Lauren any more than it drove him. It was the challenge, and in this case their mutual love of hockey. If only that shared passion could hold them together through the upheaval of the next few months.

Ethan reached across the table and took her hands, squeezing them. "Lauren, there may be a time in the not-so-distant future that it'll be hard to trust me, but just remember that I'm doing the best I can for the future of this team, even if you may not agree with my methods."

"I don't agree with the current management's methods. You listen to me. You're progressive. You're young and enthusiastic. Are they going to move the team?" Her gaze cut into his, and he didn't look away.

"I can't guarantee they'll stay in Florida."

She stared down at the contract again, and he sensed she fought a private battle between loyalty to the old guard and desperately wanting to play an active part in the new regime. Finally, she raised her head and met his gaze, nodding slowly.

"So you'll sign?"

"If you're going to be part of this team's future, I'll sign."

"I am," he admitted and handed her a pen. She wrote her name in clear, precise script and handed the contract to him.

"You won't regret this. I promise. I'll get you a copy." Ethan stuffed the contract in his briefcase and hoped she'd eventually forgive him for trapping her without giving her the full scoop on the team and its future.

The guilt overwhelmed him, even though he hadn't exactly lied about moving the team. He'd done what he had to do, and she'd hate him short-term, but it was the long-term fallout which worried him most.

* * * *

Lauren and Ethan left the restaurant and walked across the

lobby. She'd signed the contract on impulse, something she rarely did, and sealed her future with a team she knew better than she knew her family. Yet their future was as uncertain as whether or not the Giants could win three more games and make it to the Finals.

Then there was Ethan. The enigma behind the entire thing. The man with a secret. The man who made her knees weak and her heart flutter just by looking into his eyes or listening to the deep timbre of his voice—ridiculous romantic crap she'd never experienced in the past, despite the hot lust she'd once shared with her ex.

And now she'd tied herself to him for the next year. Even worse, she didn't regret signing that contract, and she'd do it again given the chance. She'd been too busy to look up the meaning of U-Dub, almost afraid to find out. Now she'd add PSHA to that list. Later. Some other day. Procrastination did have its advantages.

Lauren glanced at Ethan as they waited for the elevator, remembering another time in an elevator. He eyed her with a hungry look in his eyes as if he wanted to make her his main course.

"You're not my boss yet." The words escaped before she could stop them. Stupid, she knew, but if the Giants lost tomorrow, and she googled certain terms, everything changed between them in a split second. Then he might be her boss, but tonight he wasn't, and right now she'd twist her logic to suit her.

His blue eyes widened and desire dilated his pupils. A very sexy, very slow predatory smile eased some of the tension from his handsome face. "How do you know I will be?"

"I don't. You're not giving me any information to go on. This is a gut feeling."

"A gut feeling? From you? What about your black and white facts?" he teased and lowered his voice as he stepped closer to her, filling her nostrils with the heady scent of soap, aftershave, and man—all man.

"In a case like this, facts are highly overrated."

One eyebrow climbed into his hairline. "As in I'm not your boss tonight, so anything that might happen would be between two consulting adults?"

She laughed and stepped into the elevator. "I bet you can justify just about anything." Too much wine and not enough resistance blew her common sense into the stratosphere. What was she doing? Lauren slammed her voice of reason into a safe deposit box and let desire throw away the key. She'd signed a contract with this man, and tonight might be the last night to satisfy her cravings for Mister Tall-Dark-and-Delectable.

"When it comes to you, I can." He leaned forward, fingering her collar. "I have a suite, floors away from the team and staff. Even better, Brad isn't on this trip."

"Show me the way." Lauren's eyes feasted on his face. Just once, she wanted to see him naked. She knew enough to know he had a fine body, but she wanted to see that body without clothes in the way, to feel skin against skin, as he plunged deep inside her.

And to feel him just once, she'd abandon all common sense. For tonight.

* * * *

Ethan pulled his key card out of his wallet and jammed it in the slot several times. But each time the reader blinked red. "Damn it," he muttered. His hands shook as Lauren pried the card from his clammy fingers.

She turned the card over, inserted it, and opened the door, calm and collected. He vowed to obliterate her composure tonight and transform her into a sweaty mess, as out of control as he was. The way her eyes glowed green, he didn't think it'd prove difficult, despite the good show she put on.

She tossed the card on the desk along with her purse and turned to him. His gaze roamed down her body, over those incredible breasts confined by her business suit, past the curve of her hips, below her conservative skirt to those sexy calves and back up again until he gazed into her eyes.

She didn't look so confident now that she was in his space and out of her comfort zone. Good, he liked that. Liked that a lot. Wanted to see her composure melt along with his as they explored ecstasy together.

Hesitating, Lauren glanced at the door. Ethan paused, too, and a sliver of doubt raised its hand from the back of the room reminding him of all the reasons he shouldn't be doing this. He didn't want to be reminded so he sent his conscience packing, and let desire do the talking.

"Maybe this isn't a good idea," Lauren echoed his earlier

doubts.

Bolstered by her lack of confidence and committed to his current path no matter how stupid, Ethan moved forward and cupped her face between his hands. "I think it's a very good idea." He bent his head and ran his tongue along the curve of her neck, tasting and nibbling his way to her collarbone and back to her earlobe. He bit down on that sensitive lobe and tugged, drawing a sexy whimper from her that nearly had him losing his tenuous control.

"Maybe this is a good idea," she said breathlessly. She brought her hands up to his shoulders and stood on tiptoe to kiss him.

Ethan kissed her right back, slow and easy transforming to hot and heavy. His dick swelled to near painful proportions and pressed tight against his zipper.

"Lauren," he panted against her lips, "I have to have you. Now. Right fucking now."

"Me, too." She ran her tongue across his lips and pressed her body against his.

He stepped back far enough to unzip his jeans, but that didn't relieve the pressure mounting inside him and turning his cock painfully hard. He pushed her suit jacket off her shoulders, and she shrugged out of it, pausing to fold it and put it on a dresser.

Ethan kicked off his shoes, and shucked his shirt, jeans, and underwear with a desperation born of necessity: the necessity to bury himself in her sweet, hot wetness. As he stood naked before her, Lauren watched him with glazed eyes and said nothing. He chuckled as her gaze focused on his erection.

"Want something?"

"You." She glanced briefly at his face and downward. Like a physical caress he felt her eyes take him in, visually exploring his body.

"I like that, but you're overdressed for this party." He stepped forward to unbutton her crisp blouse, revealing an alluring pink lace bra, so very Lauren. "Do you always wear bras like this or were you expecting someone to see it tonight?"

"Both," she murmured, her voice a husky whisper that made his penis jerk in response.

She pulled off her blouse and removed her skirt.

"Holy hell. If I'd known what was hiding under your clothes, I'd have never gotten any work done." A matching pair of tiny panties, if you could even call them that, barely covered that sweet spot between her legs and didn't cover her fine ass.

"Good thing we're getting this out of the way."

"You think this'll make it easier for us to work together?"

"Absolutely not." She laughed in a rare use of profanity.

Ethan laughed, too, around the tightness in his stomach. "I want to be with you all night, Lauren, until neither one of us has the strength to move." He walked her backward to the bed and pushed her gently down onto the mattress. She clung to him, pulling him with her. He nestled his hips between her spread legs and kissed her, his tongue dancing with hers until he'd sucked the breath from her lungs.

Dragging his mouth away from her lips, he kissed his way down her neck to her chest. He took one of her distended nipples in her mouth, sucking it through the thin lace. She moaned and writhed beneath him, lifting her hips to rub against him. He sucked harder, biting down gently and tugging on her nipple with his teeth.

"That feels so good," she cried out.

"You like that, honey?" He repeated the action on her other nipple.

"Yes." She stared at him in amazement, as if she'd never felt anything like this before. He wasn't sure he had. It wasn't just physical, it was something weird and unexplainable, something scary as hell and equally as wonderful. Something with the power to elevate him to new levels or bring him to his knees and destroy him.

And all because of a little slip of a woman with her prim little suits and perfect little bun. He quirked a smile. Ah, that bun. It had to go. He lifted his head from her nipple and ran his fingers through her hair, loosening the pins and stuff that kept her hair contained until it lay in a tangled mass around her head.

The most awesome sight he'd ever seen.

Well, not exactly. Her body, her eyes, her smile were all the most awesome things he'd ever seen.

And he wanted to see more.

Reaching behind her, he unfastened her bra with flick of his fingers. He pulled the minuscule panties down past her knees, her ankles, and over the conservative heels she still wore. He sat back on his haunches and surveyed his handiwork in the form of one naked, squirming body. She was heaven gone wild.

"You're beautiful," he whispered, his words catching in his throat.

"So are you." She smiled up at him and held her arms out to him. "Come here."

"You sure are bossy when you're naked."

"I'm bossy when I'm not."

"I like bossy women."

"Show me how much you like a bossy woman." Her smirk teased him and her body tantalized him. He kissed his way down the creamy skin to her pussy, knowing foreplay would be brief this first time or he'd lose himself before he reached the final period.

"Baby, I can't hold out much longer. I'm sorry." Crawling off the bed, he fished a condom out of his wallet and rolled it on his cock while Lauren's eyes burned into him.

"Hurry up. I need you." Her throaty voice caused him to fumble with the last couple rolls of the condom.

Regardless, he was back between her legs in seconds and sinking into her warmth. She was tight, so very awesomely tight. Her muscles clenched around him, and he bit the inside of his cheek to keep from coming.

When she whimpered and squeezed her eyes shut, he froze. "Are you okay? Am I hurting you?"

"Oh, no. It feels so good, I think you're going to kill me."

"Same here, honey." Ethan pushed in bit by bit. Despite her bold words, he wanted to give her time to adjust even as he fought off his own body's protests.

Finally, Ethan was deep inside her. He held himself still, tightly leashing his passion so he didn't come on the first thrust.

Lauren refused to cooperate. She tilted her hips and pushed against him. Steeling his control, Ethan moved in and out, stroking her deeply inside, even as her body stroked his. He found her mouth and kissed her, letting her feel his hunger, unable to completely rein in the roughness. She didn't seem to mind. She clung to him, matching his rhythm, urging him to go faster and harder, until she drove him out of his effing mind.

One final thrust and her body shook, fine beads of sweat glistening on her soft skin, as she came apart and took him with her into an achingly pleasurable abyss he'd never been to with another woman. His orgasm rolled over him, wave after powerful wave and decimating in its wake every thought and every emotion that didn't pertain to her, leaving only the two of them in their world. Never alone, always together, in body and in soul.

In a moment as profound as it was powerful, she'd set him free, while at the same time ruining him for any other woman.

And he didn't care because despite all his pledges to the contrary, this woman was meant for him, and he was going to have her for his very own.

Chapter 12—Misconduct

Lauren lay in bed staring at the ceiling, her limbs like spaghetti and her muscles inoperable. Despite the heavy curtains being closed, sunlight filtered into the room, promising a beautiful spring day in Boston. After the initial euphoria of her night with Ethan, a heavy weight settled in her stomach.

Next to her, she heard Ethan's steady breathing, and her gut told her he wasn't asleep.

"This is wrong." Lauren rolled over but couldn't force herself to get out of bed.

"It doesn't feel wrong," he mumbled, his voice groggy from sleep and sounding way too content, compared to the conflict raging inside her.

He was right about that. It hadn't felt wrong. Everything about being with him had felt so right. From his silky dark hair, strong chin and passionate eyes, to his hard chest, harder cock, and his muscular thighs, it all looked and felt so right. But it was so wrong.

Ethan spooned her against him, and his erection pressed against her butt. She marveled at how quickly the man became aroused. Did every woman do that to him, or was she special? God, she wanted to be special because despite her self-righteous denials, he was special to her.

"You're practically my boss, or you could be in the future."

"But I'm not. Not yet. Right now we're partners at best. We talked about this. No regrets, Lauren. No repercussions. Nothing. To demonstrate I'm an honorable man, I'll tear up the contract if that's what you want."

And let go of all that money? More money than she'd made in her last ten years with the Giants. She could get a fresh start, maybe make a down payment on a little house with a backyard and a garden. She could get a dog and not listen to her neighbors flush their toilets. She could BBQ on the back porch while the birds chirped and actually have her own trees. Even more, she could stay in Ethan's life, work side by side with him to build a team to be reckoned with, and if she dared to dream, perhaps, have a future with him.

Stupid thoughts from a woman who'd been through this before and had lost her abundant common sense when it came to another good-looking, blue-eyed man.

Yet she couldn't walk away from her dream job or this man, despite the questionable wisdom of such a decision. All he asked was a year. These opportunities didn't come her way more than once a lifetime.

Even so, she needed more assurance, as she'd been played for a fool once before and it'd devastated her financially and emotionally along with obliterating her confidence in her ability to make the correct choices. Being played a fool by Max had almost ruined her, being played a fool by Ethan would cause irreparable destruction to her heart.

"I don't want you to tear it up. But what do we do when you're my boss?"

"I don't know." He rolled onto his back and pulled her across his chest as he stared at the ceiling.

"You don't know?" She hadn't expected his answer. The Ethan she knew had all the answers.

"This is uncharted territory for me."

"You've never done this before?"

Pain flickered briefly in his eyes. "Only once," he whispered, "but it didn't feel like this. Nothing has ever felt like this."

Lauren squeezed her eyes shut and attempted to staunch the flow of tears.

He couldn't see how much his words affected her, nor could she hope he meant what he said.

* * * *

The Giants won game five to stay alive in the semis with a last minute goal by winger Drew Delacorte. They'd need to win the next two to advance to the Finals. After a late-night flight back home, Lauren hauled her tired ass to work with only a few hours of sleep. Ethan looked as rough as she felt. For once she didn't work late, but left for home at five to catch up on much needed sleep. Ethan and she didn't say much to each other, keeping it strictly business, even though she suspected he wanted to discuss their night together. Thankfully, he kept his mouth shut and gave her space.

Twenty minutes after she arrived home, Lauren's father walked into her apartment without knocking. Her fault—she should've locked the door. Lon seated himself at the tiny dining room table, his bulk taking up the majority of the small room. She automatically poured him a cup of coffee. He drank the stuff twenty-four-seven.

Waiting him out and knowing he couldn't be hurried, she tidied up her living room and kitchen, poured herself a glass of wine, and rifled through her mail.

Lon stretched, yawned, and rubbed his chin. "I've been doing research."

"Is this where I'm supposed to ask you what you're researching?" She sighed.

"Don't be a smartass, Lauren." He leveled one of those go-stand-in-the-corner looks at her. Only that look didn't work anymore.

When she didn't react, he continued. "I can't find anything on Ethan Williams as far as being who he is and what he is. I've found plenty on another Ethan. Ethan Parker. The man behind the mirror of the group who's been trolling for a hockey team to move to Seattle. His family has billions."

Lauren went cold inside. "That's not him."

"Are you certain?" Her father's eyes narrowed, and he saw much more than she wanted him to see. "You're sleeping with him. Every time you sleep with a guy, you lose your objectivity."

"That only happened once, Dad."

"Once should've taught you a lesson. Max was sleeping with puck bunnies in every town he played in. We all told you that, but you wouldn't believe us."

She hadn't wanted to believe her friends and family, not until she'd followed Max to Boston and pounded on the door of his hotel room, finding him with the women. Now she was playing the denial card with Ethan.

"Lauren, you're susceptible to smooth-talking bastards."

"Ethan is not a bastard. He has the same passion for hockey that you and I share."

Lon gaped at her as if she'd hit her head on the ice and had a concussion. "Honey, Ethan does not have a passion for the game. Not like us. He's not a—"

"—Hockey guy? Dad, I know. I thought so myself, but he is. He loves hockey. Do you realize that he skates with Cooper every morning?"

"Are you serious?" Lon shook his head in absolute disbelief, as if he'd been the one to slam his head into the ice and lose his senses.

"He does." She hoped she wasn't revealing a fact about Ethan's character that Ethan wouldn't appreciate.

"You're not going to give me any info that'll help my group's cause, are you, Lauren? That ass has you wrapped around his finger, and he's using you."

Lauren bristled, poised to defend the man she loved.

Her head reeled. Her stomach twisted. Her heart slammed in her chest.

What the hell? Loved?

She couldn't love Ethan. Hell, she'd loved before and been taken on a ride she'd never forget. This girl didn't do stupid twice, or maybe she already had. She'd slept with him, signed a contract without even knowing who was really employing her, and she'd given him her heart.

Her father studied her as if trying to read her mind. She sat up straighter, slipped into businesslike-bitch mode, and looked him in the eyes. "So tell me, Dad. What position would I have with the team if your group bought it?" Nothing like laying it on the line with the old man.

Lon didn't answer right away. Instead he looked at a spot over her head as if her cheap print of flowers hanging on the wall were a priceless piece of art. He fidgeted, glanced at his watch, and fidgeted some more.

"Dad?" she nudged him for a response.

"You'd keep the position you have, of course."

"Would that be the position that my title indicates I have or the one I really have?"

"Lauren, I can't speak to that. I'm the front man, but it's not my money."

"That answers my question, Dad."

"Honey, you have to understand my group is composed of men who've lived and breathed hockey their entire lives. They'll have a say in who does what with the organization, but don't worry, I've made sure that there's a place saved just for you."

Lauren saw the handwriting on the wall. This group would be even worse than the current group of good ol' boys. "What happens to the coaching staff?"

"You know how I feel about them, hon. They aren't quite championship caliber. The team we field will have the best coaches money can buy."

There'd be no place for a woman in her father's hierarchy. Even if her father forced that hierarchy to accept her, they wouldn't put her in any kind of position with any say in the organization.

But Ethan would. Ethan who'd hinted at moving the team, avoided the tough questions, and worst case scenario happened to be Ethan Parker.

Lauren closed her eyes for a moment, steeling herself against her father's wrath, and told the truth. "I'm going to work for Ethan's group if they get the team, Dad. I'm sorry. I hope you don't see it as a betrayal because it's not. He's promised me what I've longed for all these years, an actual say in the running of the team." And a shitload of money, but if she told her father that right now, he'd assume Ethan was essentially paying her to sleep with him.

He wasn't. Absolutely was not. She believed in Ethan. She had to. Her future rode on his broad shoulders. She didn't trust easily, but he'd earned her trust.

Her father's eyes hardened, causing her stomach to clench, but she held strong. Lon stood and walked to the door, his back stiff, his stride tight. He turned to her as he opened the door. "I hope to God you know what you're doing, Lauren, and that man is worth losing the respect of the staff and your family." Without another word, he walked out and shut the door with an ominous click.

Lauren stared at the closed door for what seemed a lifetime but was actually about fifteen minutes. A lone tear escaped down her cheek. She swiped at it, picked up her phone, and called her aunt— the one person in the world who could make sense of all this without passing judgment, probably because she'd had judgment passed on her too many times.

Aunt Jo answered on the fifth ring, just before Lauren was about to give up. "Hey, my beautiful niece, what's up?"

"I need your wise counsel."

Aunt Jo chuckled. "Counsel I can give. Wise, not so sure, but hit me. I'll do my best."

Lauren ran through the events of the past month, not leaving much untold, well, except for the getting naked part. Aunt Jo, true to form, listened and made no comment until Lauren finished.

"So what are your concerns?"

"Am I selling out my family for money? Am I being an idiot like I was with Max?"

"I can't tell you that. You know the answer in your heart, just like you knew Max was a sweet-talking man-whore."

"But I did it anyway just to show my father I could do what I wanted."

Her aunt chuckled. "Your father is living in the old world, one which will pass him by in short order. You're part of the future, Lauren. Make sure you contribute to it; don't add to its postponement. You're a savvy hockey person with an eye for talent and for details. You know what makes a winner, but to date no one has given you credit for that knowledge and the gift you have for recognizing talent. But it sounds like your Ethan has."

"He's not my Ethan."

"For the next short while, he might be."

"I don't know."

"Lauren, abandoning the old and comfortable takes guts. Following a new path, one that rings true is worth the risk if you believe it is, no matter the outcome."

"The money is guaranteed."

"That's a plus, but this isn't about the money, and we both know that. It's about respect for who and what you are, and I know a helluva lot about that. Your father didn't accept me and my personal choices for years. The only reason he tolerated me is because he had three kids to take care of and a job that required a lot of traveling. I took over his personal responsibilities, not that I didn't adore being part of the family because I did, and I love my kids."

"I know. Dad was never a hands-on father, not when Mom lived with us and not after she left. His marriage and his family are hockey. As long as the three of us translated into hockey, we could be in his sphere."

"It was toughest on you, Lauren."

"I never could quite measure up to his expectations because I wasn't born with a dick and no matter how hard I tried, I couldn't be what the boys were."

"But you could be as good in a different way." Jo hesitated, and continued cautiously, as if choosing her words carefully. "I love my brother to death. He's gruff, behind-the-times, and stubborn beyond belief, but I still love him, just as you do. Sometimes, the best thing for all parties is the hardest thing. You need to get out from under his shadow and find out who Lauren is. Ethan respects you for your knowledge and skills, not for who your father and brothers are."

"I think he does." Lauren took a deep breath and plunged in with the rest. "But I've slept with him. That changes everything."

Jo was so quiet for so long, Lauren suspected she'd hung up. "Obviously, you're attracted to him and he is to you. Is there more to it than that?"

"I don't know. I'm worried I'm falling in love with him. I never thought I'd be able to love after Max, yet this is different. More mature. Not just based on a physical attraction."

"You'd be surprised how your thinking changes when the right person drops into your lap."

"I don't know if he's the right person or the very wrong person, but I'm in deeper than I ever planned to be."

"Good thing you're a strong swimmer. Instead of swimming for a safe but boring shore, head for that distant island paradise. Take the risk. You never know where it might lead."

Lauren considered her aunt's words for a moment. "Thanks, Aunt Jo. I appreciate your advice."

"You're welcome. I'm only a phone call away."

They said their goodbyes and Lauren hung up, still not certain if the paradise she swam toward was real or a mirage. Regardless, she'd committed to it, and she'd keep swimming in that direction hoping Ethan would send a lifeboat to rescue her.

Choosing Ethan wouldn't bode well for her family relationships in the future, but surely they'd get over it. Her brothers and father had made choices in their lives that put their family second to their careers. Just because she was a woman didn't mean she should always put family first, even if they did see it that way.

Ethan was her future, even if she wasn't certain to what extent, but who the hell was Ethan?

Crossing to her laptop sitting on the small desk in the living room, Lauren sat down and flipped it open. It hummed to life. Her fingers hovered over the keyboard as she ran through the terms she needed to Google: *UDub, PSHA, Ethan Parker.*

PSHA turned up pages and pages of hits for various companies and by page ten, she gave up. She had better luck with U-Dub, which was Seattle natives' nickname for The University of Washington. Ethan must have attended college in Seattle, which tied him to the city.

Her heart lodged in her throat while her stomach churned at the possibility. Ethan Parker. The billionaire attempting to poach an NHL team and move it to Seattle? Her Ethan? All the pieces fit like a custom pair of skates. To deny the obvious would be beyond stupid.

Yet she'd worked side-by-side with Ethan for a few months and spent almost every waking hour sharing their dreams for the Giants. She'd fallen in love with him despite all intentions to the contrary, and she'd put her trust in him when she didn't think she'd ever trust another man again. Even if he was Ethan Parker, she believed he would listen to her as he had all along and give the Gainesville Giants a chance to stay in Florida.

Lauren shut down the laptop without typing another character.

Whoever Ethan really was—savior or sinner—she didn't want to know. Not yet.

* * * *

Ethan glanced around Lauren's apartment complex. No one was out and about. The sun was setting and the place was damn quiet. He raised his hand and rapped on the door.

Holding his breath, he waited.

He'd tried to stay away but couldn't. Lauren drew him to her like a magnet to iron, and he needed her like he'd never needed another woman.

He'd been taken for a fool before, assuming Danielle had been trustworthy and cared about him for who he was. What made him think his judgment regarding any woman's true intentions had improved over the past few years? Danielle did her damnedest to ruin his reputation and take some of his hard-earned money with her. He'd paid her off to shut her up, only to have her marry a friend of his a few months later as she laughed all the way to the bank. She'd played him for a sucker, which really irritated him since he hadn't done any of the things she'd accused him of doing. Regardless, he'd been guilty of sleeping with her when she'd been in his employ. That'd been enough.

Now he was making the same mistake twice, only with Lauren it didn't feel like a mistake.

So here he stood, a bouquet of flowers in one hand and a tentative smile on his face, hoping against hope she wouldn't boot his ass to the parking lot.

Lauren opened the door, as if expecting him, her smile as tentative as his. Her eyes zeroed in on the flowers and her hands flew upward to cover her mouth. He wasn't sure if her reaction was a good thing or a bad thing.

"May I come in?" he asked with stiff politeness.

"Yes, you may," she parroted back, but a smile tugged at one corner of her mouth, and her eyes sparkled a deep green, giving him a shot of confidence. She *was* happy to see him on her doorstep, and he sure as hell was happy to see her.

Ethan entered the small but tidy little apartment and glanced around. She wasn't much for decorating. A few nondescript scenery prints hung on the walls here and there. Her furniture consisted of a worn couch and an equally worn overstuffed leather chair, along with bistro table in the dining area. Obviously, the woman didn't spend much time here.

A very fat, fluffy gray cat lolled on the chair and opened one green eye to watch him, as if to say, don't you dare take my chair, buddy.

Ethan turned his attention back to Lauren who stood quietly beside him. "I didn't know you had a cat."

"I don't. Not exactly. He belongs to my neighbors, but he likes me better."

"Smart cat." He held the bouquet out to her. "These are for you."

She took them from him and inhaled deeply. "They smell wonderful, but you didn't have to do that."

"I wanted to." He leaned against the counter as she put the flowers in water and placed the vase on the table. He watched as her compact, athletic body—one he'd seen naked two nights ago—moved with an easy grace across the room.

Unable to resist, Ethan caught her around the waist and pulled her to him, kissing her with a hunger only she could satisfy. She buried her fingers in his hair and kissed him right back with such intensity he swore their mouths would be bruised.

Finally, panting, he drew back slightly and gazed into her eyes. That simple act of looking through that window into a person's soul struck him deep down inside. In a profound moment of clarity, he knew, as sure as he knew his own name, Lauren was special to him and to his future, and he'd protect what they had with a fierceness he'd only reserved for family in the past.

She was an essential part of his plan, personal and professional, and he'd be damned if he'd let her go, even if rocky times were ahead. Somehow he'd find a way to show her that despite his deception, he meant well and deserved to be forgiven.

Tonight would be a start, a prelude to the storm about to crash down on them as soon as the Giants played their final game, which could be as early as tomorrow and as late as a month or so. The Sleezers were peeing their pants in anticipation of cashing Ethan's big check, and they wouldn't wait a millisecond longer than necessary.

Lauren brought a finger up to his lips. "What are you thinking? You seem so serious."

"I'm always serious. That's why I've been Brad's straight man all these years, going back to high school."

"There's nothing wrong with serious, but you should laugh more."

He tucked a lock of brown hair behind her ear. "I've laughed more this past month with you than I have in years. I guess I take life too seriously."

"Ditto." She smiled up at him, and he grinned like a fool.

"We both need to live a little less seriously. We could start tonight. In bed. You and me. An encore presentation."

"I love encores."

"I love you naked."

"You're not so hard on the eyes yourself." She slid her hands up under his T-shirt and along his ribcage. "I think you're wearing entirely too many clothes for a hot night like this."

"I think you're right." He lifted his arms over his head and let her pull off his shirt. She tossed it aside, walked him backward to the couch and stopped when the back of his knees bumped the seat. Lauren put her hands on his belt, and he sucked in a deep breath, holding it while she unbuckled his belt and slid his jeans past his hips and down his thighs. Ethan kicked off his shoes and stepped out of his jeans.

She leisurely perused his body, and he stood completely still. Her gaze felt so hot it was almost as if she were touching him. Then she did touch him, and his knees buckled. He sat down hard on the couch, while she knelt in front of him. Placing her hands on his inner thighs, she gently spread them to make room between his legs. Lauren ran her hands up his thighs and cupped him through his underwear, gently squeezing him. Ethan groaned, like the happy groan of a man on his way to heaven.

Her silky hair slid across his belly as she ran a tongue across his flat stomach and dipped it in his navel. He lifted his hips off the couch when she tugged on his waistband and pulled down his briefs to free his erection.

Lauren gawked unabashedly at his dick and licked her lips. Ethan tilted his head back against the couch and shut his eyes, gritting his teeth, while forcing himself to show patience he didn't have. She bent her head and licked the tip. His hips jerked, and he gripped the seat cushions in a futile attempt to keep himself on earth when any moment he might be launched into space by her touch.

She ran her fingertip up the prominent vein in his cock, over the tip, and back down to his balls. Lowering her head, she put her mouth on him and bobbed her head up and down, taking him deep into her wet mouth and driving him fucking nuts.

When he couldn't take anymore and was about to come in her mouth, he lifted her upward, despite her protests.

"I need to be inside you, honey."

Through heavily lidded eyes she regarded him and nodded, stripping off her clothes in record time.

"Condom?"

"In my jeans pocket."

Lauren pulled several out of his pocket and raised one eyebrow at him He grinned. She tore open one packet, sliding it over his erection in a few efficient tugs. She sat back on her haunches, admiring her handiwork. Ethan placed his hands on her waist and lifted her onto his lap, guiding her down on his dick until he was fully seated inside her.

God, she felt like every fantasy he'd ever had about how a woman should feel and far better than any real woman he'd been inside. Lauren was uniquely his in the way they fit together.

She leaned forward, her hands perched on his shoulders, and kissed the hell out of him. She started riding him, slowly at first, but picking up speed and intensity with each stroke. She drove him out of his mind until he couldn't think of anything but her and didn't know his own name, but he sure as hell knew hers. She grabbed his hands and leaned way back, changing the angle and driving him even deeper inside her.

The climax thundered through his body, starting in his core and extending out to his arms and legs until every part of his body was involved along with his brain and his soul. Lauren closed her eyes and her muscles clenched tight around his dick as she followed him to completion.

Sometime later—he didn't know how long because time didn't exist where she'd sent him—he began to be aware of their bodies entwined while the cat sat on the back of the couch and flicked its tail in his face.

Finally Lauren rolled off him and blinked a few times as if to orient herself. Ethan stood, picked her up, and carried her to the bedroom, knowing that it'd be another sleepless night for the two of them, but he wouldn't have it any other way.

At least, he'd brought plenty of condoms.

* * * *

Ethan was uncharacteristically late the next morning, and so was Lauren. Hell, he even missed his skate with Cooper, which he did somewhat regret. Brad was waiting for him when he walked into the office at the Giants facility. His buddy scowled in a very atypical Brad way. In fact, his expression reminded Ethan of the same one Ethan's father wore after Ethan had snuck out at night as a teenager and gotten wasted drunk.

"What's stuck up your ass?" Ethan said, taking a seat at his desk and waking up his laptop.

"Damn, E, you're smarter than this. Didn't you learn your lesson a few years ago?" Brad didn't waste time on niceties or small talk, just got right to the point. Not usually Brad's MO, but he appeared to be that irritated.

"I've learned a shitload of lessons. Which one might you be referring to?" Ethan feigned ignorance.

"There's something going on with you and Lauren." Brad perched his hands on his hips and leaned over Ethan's desk.

Ethan smiled up at him, keeping his voice level. "Ah, that. Don't miss much, do you?"

"It's hard to miss. Everyone's suspicious. Not just me."

"For the record, she's not my employee. She's an employee of the Giants."

"You're splitting hairs. What's the league going to say if this gets out? What if she sues you?"

"She won't. I'm ninety-nine percent certain she's not that type of woman."

"You said the same thing about the last woman you had on the payroll and between the sheets. That one percent is a killer, E."

"You make it sound like I make a habit out of this."

"You're getting close in my book. Two women in two years doesn't say much for your track record."

Ethan growled, hating that Brad might well be right. "And I'm friends with you why?"

"Because of my magnetic personality and unparalleled charisma. You can't help yourself." Finally Brad grinned his trademark cocky grin. He'd never been one to stay mad long, even when Ethan deserved it.

"You're like a bad habit I can't shake."

"I've been told that before, but usually by women." Brad snorted. Nothing got under his skin, except his oldest brother who happened to be the world's biggest tight ass or had been until he'd been loosened up by a woman. Funny what the right woman could do to a guy.

"I want to tell her, Brad. Tell her everything."

"You can't. We're so close, buddy. Remember the gag order. You cannot tell her."

"Look, I'm going to do what I have to do. I know what I'm doing." Ethan prayed he truly did. "So don't worry about me or the team, okay? I can handle it."

Brad studied his friend for a long moment. "I hope so, E, I truly hope so."

So did Ethan.

Chapter 13—Major Penalty

Ethan had never wanted anything as much as he wanted the Giants to win the semi-finals and advance to the Cup Finals. Not just because the Cup was the ultimate prize, but because it'd postpone the eventual disaster that'd arise from the announcement of the team's sale to a group of Seattle investors, and it'd postpone the inevitable with Lauren. She'd be pissed as hell, and he couldn't blame her.

That next evening the team took the ice for what might be their last home game in this arena as the Giants. They won, thanks again to the superb play of Cedric and Cooper, and tied the series at three to three. Early the next morning they flew to Boston for game seven. It all came down to one game in order to decide who played in the Finals.

Ethan had spent the last few nights with Lauren, knowing each night could be their last for the foreseeable future. Every possible scenario about the outcome of their relationship ended with her being pissed as hell at him and murdering him in his sleep. None of it was pretty.

When the coach knocked on his hotel suite a few hours before the team was bussed to the arena, Ethan took one look at the man's face and sensed his carefully laid plans were about to come crashing down, and there might not be a damn thing he could do to stop the carnage.

"Come in, Coach. What can I do for you?" Ethan stretched, wearily rubbing the back of his neck. These marathon sex sessions with Lauren were killing his sleep. The coach walked past him into the room and stood in front of the big windows, hands clasped behind his back as he stared out at the city.

Ethan stiffened, preparing for the worst while attempting to remain casual. "Could I get you a cup of coffee?"

"This isn't a social visit." His hands fisted at his sides, Coach kept his back to Ethan.

"I see." Ethan poured himself a cup of strong, black coffee, fearing he'd need it.

The coach turned to face him, hands propped on his hips, his eyes blazing with anger. "I know who you are, Parker."

Ethan drew in a breath and let it out. His brain raced ahead in a futile attempt to find a solution before this blew up in his face. "I'm not sure what you're talking about." Not exactly an epic response, but Ethan needed more information.

"Does Puget Sound Hockey Alliance mean anything to you?" Coach raised one eyebrow as his lips lifted in a sneer.

Again Ethan refused to respond, even as his mind churned with questions he didn't dare ask.

"This team is headed for Seattle, isn't it?" The coach studied Ethan.

"You have a game to win in a couple hours. I think this discussion is best left until later."

"I want this team to skate for the Cup. I wouldn't do anything to sabotage that. But let me make one thing clear. I'm not moving to Seattle."

Ethan had news for Fur. He didn't plan on keeping him on as head coach, but he let the man save face. He'd actually just solved one of Ethan's problems by his statement. "Assuming this team is moving to Seattle, you aren't going with it?"

"I just said that, didn't I? I know all about you and your group. I know the deal is already done but the league doesn't want anyone to know. I know there's an opening in Arizona for a coach, and I'm taking it."

"If that's what you want." Ethan asked the question that'd been burning through him ever since Fur entered the room. "How did you find out?"

"I have friends in the league office. They didn't want me to miss out on this coaching opportunity, which I would've never considered if the team were staying in Florida."

"I see. It's imperative this not get out until the team plays its last game."

"You don't need to worry about me. I'm not telling a damn soul. That's your problem." Fur turned and slammed the door as he left.

Ethan stared at the closed door, knowing it was only a matter of time. Tonight, win or lose, he'd tell Lauren so she'd hear it from him and no one else, and he could put a positive spin on it while begging her forgiveness.

* * * *

Lauren sat in the stands, not moving, not talking, not doing a thing. The Giants playoff run was over, and she was numb.

Finally she glanced at Ethan sitting next to her. Stone-faced, he stared unblinking at the celebration on the ice, oblivious to the cheering fans rocking the arena all around them.

Lauren's heart went out to the Giants who'd played so hard to get this far. Cooper picked himself up off the ice where he'd been slammed against the boards. Head down, he waited with his teammates in a line to congratulate the winners of a hard-fought game then the team exited the ice and headed for the locker room. Lauren wanted to console each and every one of them, but nothing she might say would make this hurt any less.

Long after the fans began to disperse, Lauren and Ethan sat in silence. Finally, Lauren grabbed Ethan's hand and squeezed it.

"It's over," she said.

He turned to her. Determination etched on his handsome face. "No, it's just begun. This team is under new ownership now."

"It is?" Lauren was taken aback by the finality of his statement, as if this were a done deal.

"To my knowledge, the team is sold."

"It'll be an interesting era without the Sleezers." Lauren studied him with his furrowed brow and troubled eyes.

"Yes, it will. I promise things will be better if you give us a chance." He pleaded with her to understand something she wasn't sure she wanted to understand.

"I'm on board. I signed that contract, didn't I?" It was time to leave the old ways behind and usher in new ones. Despite the loss, she should be excited over her new role with the team, but Ethan's guilty expression dampened her excitement.

"Lauren, it's about to get worse before it gets better."

"I believe in you, Ethan. You are a hockey guy."

He smiled at her words, even though his eyes didn't smile. "That's the finest compliment I've ever received." Blowing out a breath, he stared down at their intertwined fingers. "There's something you need to know. Something I have to tell you, and I want you to hear it from me."

"Not now, not here."

He nodded. "Let's go somewhere private."

"Okay." Lauren stood and so did Ethan.

It wouldn't be long before he told her the entire story, and his words would change everything, and she didn't want things to change. She wanted to bottle the past several weeks of memories and keep them forever, moments in time to be replayed over and over, with no bad ending. In fact, no ending at all.

But an ending was coming—an ending Lauren had foreseen but denied, and there was nothing she could do to change it. Instead she put her faith in Ethan one more time.

* * * *

Side by side, Ethan and Lauren navigated to the bowels of the building and the locker room area. Ethan was determined to get Lauren alone as soon as possible and tell her everything. The press bustled around them, pushing and shoving to get near players for interviews and photos.

Ethan gently held Lauren's elbow to stop them from being separated in the crowd.

Brad appeared out of the sea of people and grabbed his arm. "Ethan, we need to talk."

Ethan hesitated, reluctant to leave Lauren's side when she was so devastated over the team's loss. It might be one of their last nights together before the truth came out and revealed him for the fraud he was. He wanted to savor their relationship a little longer and be the one to tell her the truth, try to lessen the blow, and hope she understood his reasons.

"*Now.*" Happy-go-lucky Brad growled in a manner Ethan couldn't recall ever hearing.

He bent his head close to Lauren's. "Where will you be?"

"I'll wait in the small office off the visitors' locker room."

"I won't be long. We can drown our sorrows."

"At least we still have each other." She stood on tiptoe to kiss his cheek. Her sad smile tugged at his heart and compounded his guilt. She knew. He was certain of it. At the least, she suspected. Why the fuck hadn't he told her sooner, and to hell with the league?

Brad didn't even blink, didn't tease him, didn't say a damn thing. Instead he hauled him into the equipment room, booting out the equipment guys.

"Don't fucking tell me the league changed their minds?" Ethan clenched and unclenched his jaw, unable to shake the sensation of standing on the verge of a disaster.

"The Sleezers are in a press conference right now. I heard part of it. They announced the team has been sold and will be moving to Seattle. In a matter of minutes, it'll be all over the Internet."

As he paced the floor, Ethan erupted in a rare burst of colorful obscenities including a few created just for this occasion. "The coach already figured it out. He quit a few hours before the game. His resignation effective after they played their last game."

"Which they just did," Brad said grimly.

"Yeah, they did. I knew it was going to get out, and Coach promised he'd wait for the official announcement."

"He kept his word, but the Sleezeballs didn't," Brad ground out between gritted teeth, his devil-may-care attitude turned into a bust-someone's-face attitude.

"I knew they wouldn't wait long—they wanted their money—but I never thought they'd make the announcement without warning me so I could do damage control."

"There's no damage to control when everything's been blown to pieces. One bright spot, the Sleezers effectively negated any hope of a competing offer."

That didn't make Ethan feel any better. "I need to talk to Lauren..." He rushed for the door, Brad hot on his heels.

"No time for that." Brad yanked him around. "Get in that locker room. Give them the speech we rehearsed."

"I need to talk to Lauren." His voice took on a desperate tone.

"You need to talk to the team, reassure them. I'll do the same thing with the staff."

Ethan nodded. As much as he hated it, Brad was right. It couldn't be helped. Not one damn bit. They only had seconds before this thing blew up, if it hadn't already. He ran his hand through his hair and sighed, trudging toward the locker room while Brad trudged to the gallows in the opposite direction.

Drawing in a deep breath, Ethan strolled through the door, ready to do battle by presenting a calm, strong front in the face of adversity.

Several long faces glanced up at him as he entered. As a whole, each face hardened to stone. The hatred in their eyes set Ethan back on his heels, but now was not the time to demonstrate weakness. Coach stood center stage, hands on hips.

They already knew.

Ethan strode up to the middle of the room, careful not to step on the logo of a team no longer in existence.

"Coach, I'm guessing you've told the team about the ownership change?"

Coach nodded, his jaw tight, his eyes angry. "I told them. They're your team now. Good luck. You'll need it." He stomped from the room and slammed the door so hard the room shook.

A pleasant smile plastered his face, Ethan directed his attention on the team. "Hello, gentlemen..."

No one said a thing.

"I apologize for not being honest, but I had to do it not by choice, but by necessity.

Not a word. They continued to glare at him.

"It wasn't supposed to go down like this. I regret the announcement happened without careful planning."

"Planning? Bullshit. You could take months to announce it, and the result would be the same." Cooper's blue eyes hardened to angry slits. His boys backed him up with similar angry expressions. Even good-natured Cedric glared at Ethan.

"I'm not sure how much the coach told you, but I'm Ethan Parker, majority owner and president of this organization, known as the Seattle Sockeyes from this point forward. My investors are Seattle natives with a love for sports and community. We may not be hockey guys in the strictest sense of the word, but we have a passion to produce a winning team and start a legacy of hockey in Seattle and make this team a contender year after year."

"How are you going to do that?" Matt LeRue, one of the other team captains, said with a thick French Canadian accent that only came out when he was stressed or pissed off.

"We'll be assembling the best support team possible from progressive hockey minds. We'll build a team of players who mesh well together. If you perform well, I promise you'll be paid well within the constraints of the salary cap."

A couple of the guys leaned forward until Cooper shot them a murderous glare with pounds of threat behind it. They stared at their feet and said nothing.

Cooper challenged him. "It's not all about the money. Is it, guys?" Nods and murmurs of agreement accompanied his words.

"Everything will be first class. The practice facility, the staff, the coaches, the workout room, the food. Everything. No expense will be spared. We'll be a progressive team—our methods might be unorthodox, but all options are on the table as far as I'm concerned."

"What about integrity and trust? Is that still on the table?" Cooper stood, hands on hips, legs slightly apart. His chin jutted out and his eyes shone with belligerence. Several other guys stood to show their support. Cedric and Matt flanked Cooper.

Ethan deserved that question, but he couldn't admit it and show an ounce of weakness. Nor could he explain why he'd been deceptive. The league wouldn't appreciate him spilling the beans about the gag order. Pissing off the commissioner would start his ownership off on the wrong foot.

"I'm sorry. I didn't have a choice. We couldn't announce the sale before your season ended. I didn't want to mess with the magic you had going here."

Cooper rolled his eyes. "That's bullshit. You don't give a shit about magic or us. You were thinking of the bottom line. The further we skated into the playoffs, the better this team looks to your investors and the new city. It's all about the money."

Ethan didn't see a point in continuing this conversation until the team had time to process what just happened, and Cooper had time to cool off. He swept his gaze around the room, calmly assessing each player. Some glowered back in silent challenge, others stared at the floor.

"Welcome to the Sockeyes' organization, gentlemen. Give us a chance. Give Seattle a chance. You'll love it there." Ethan left before they could shoot him or his city down.

He was halfway down the hall when Cooper grabbed his arm, angrier than Ethan had ever seen him. "What the hell? I thought you were an okay guy. I was starting to trust you, but you used me."

Ethan stared into Cooper's eyes, brimming with fury and a hint of hurt. "I wasn't using you. I'm sorry I wasn't straight with you. I couldn't be. Give me a chance, Coop, to make this right."

"The only way you can make this right is to get the hell out of here and leave this team where it is."

"I won't do that. This team moves to Seattle."

"Then you and I have nothing to discuss. Trade me."

"I won't do that either. You're under contract for one more year. You are a Sockeye, like it or not."

"I don't like it."

"Tough shit." It was Ethan's turn to walk away after having the last word.

Cooper would come around eventually because when it came down to it, he just wanted to play hockey.

It was Lauren Ethan worried about. And he had to find her right now.

* * * *

Something was wrong. Horribly wrong, and it had nothing to do with losing the game. The din outside the small room went beyond a playoff loss for the Giants. Lauren opened the door and pushed her way through the throng of excited reporters crowded around Brad. They were shooting rapid-fire questions at him, talking over each other in their frenzy to get a scoop. She tapped one national reporter she knew pretty well on the arm. He turned around to face her.

"Bob, what's going on?"

"You didn't know either? This had to be the best-kept secret in all of pro sports."

"What secret? Bob, tell me now." Her heart sank to her toes with dread.

"The team has been sold and is being moved to Seattle. It's a done deal. The coach has been fired, and they'll probably clean house with the remaining staff and coaches."

"Who bought them?" She gripped his arm so tight he glared at her and yanked it away.

"Bunch of wealthy Seattle investors headed up by billionaire Ethan Parker, one of the richest families in Seattle, and there's a lot of rich guys in Seattle so that tells you a lot. The man has more money than God."

"I knew it," Lauren whispered. Denial was no longer an option.

"Hope you like rain, Lauren. Look, I have to file this story. Later."

Lauren stood alone in a sea of humanity and had never felt so alone. She'd known the truth just like she'd know the truth about

Max, but she'd stayed in her little cocoon of blissful ignorance until the reality of the situation bit her in the ass.

Ethan had used her, played her for a fool, and hadn't even had the decency to tell her about this himself before all hell broke loose. Sure, he'd tried to tell her tonight, but what about all those other nights? Why hadn't he trusted her enough to confide in her? That hurt more than the team's relocation and his dishonesty.

Lauren ran for the exit, needing to get out of there and as far away from Ethan as she could, but Ethan stepped from the shadows and stopped her, holding her by the arms so she couldn't escape. She stared at him, too angry to form a coherent word.

"Lauren, I'm sorry. I wanted to tell you so many times. I really did."

"Sure you did. You didn't trust me. You thought I'd tell my father."

"No, it's not that. I do trust you."

"Then you didn't want to ruin a good thing. I gave you my honest opinion about the staff, players, and coaches. Are you going to use that against them?"

"Lauren, I won't lie to you—"

"Well, that's a welcome change."

"Most of what you told me only verified my own conclusions. Things will change for the better. We're committed to putting out a competitive product year after year."

"You fired Coach."

"I didn't fire him. He quit."

"He probably saw the handwriting on the wall."

"He probably did, Lauren."

"What about my dad? Is he gone, too?"

"I'd like to keep him. He's one of the best scouts in the business."

"There's one person you don't need to worry about firing. I quit."

Ethan's sad expression almost made her feel sorry for him. "You can't quit; you signed a contract."

"Under false pretenses."

"I need you, Lauren," Ethan pleaded, his blue eyes luminous as if this were as upsetting to him as it was to her.

"You don't need me. There are plenty of others willing to take my place with your precious Sockeyes and in your bed. And they won't mind the rain."

"Lauren, please. Give Seattle and the organization a chance."

"I will not. I've been burned once by a dishonest man. I believed every one of his lies, and the truth ripped out my heart. I barely put it back together. I can't go through this again, and I won't." Tears filled her eyes, and she started sniffling. Lauren wiped her eyes on her sleeve.

"I care about you, Lauren. I want to make this work." His earnest gaze almost sucked her into his web, but she resisted.

"Go to hell. Tear up my contract." She embraced her anger because it held back her tears.

His face hardened and his blue eyes frosted over. He wasn't going to back down. She could almost hear him dig in his heels. "I didn't want it to be like this between us. You want to play hard ball? We'll play hardball."

"Hit me with your best shot," she challenged him, knowing she'd just waved a red flag in front of a charging bull.

"Do you have the money to take me to court?" he said in an infuriatingly calm, businesslike voice.

Lauren didn't, and the bastard knew it.

"I didn't think so. See you in Seattle, Lauren."

"Fuck you."

Regret tinged with sadness flickered in his eyes. "I'll see you at work in your new office two weeks from Monday. My assistant will contact you and the rest of the staff with information on housing and moving expenses." Ethan strode off, his spine straight and his head held high.

Lauren wanted to find a place to cry. She'd fallen for the jerk, and he'd screwed her over. It might not have been with another woman like it had been with Max, but Ethan's betrayal was just as painful and damaging. Actually, it was worse.

She'd never trust him again. Ever. She'd work until her contract ended and not a minute more, take his money, pay off her debts, and somehow find another team willing to give a woman a chance.

Lauren walked out of the arena, hailed a cab, and went to the airport to fly back to Florida one last time before she left the sunshine for the rain.

On cue, rain started to fall and nothing but gray loomed ahead.

Chapter 14—Shootout

The next day, Ethan sat in conference room at a Gainesville hotel across the table from the commissioner, who'd flown in that morning. Cyrus, his ever-faithful and ever-ruthless attorney sat on his right and Brad, on his left. They wouldn't be leaving this office until the league blessed his purchase.

"The team is mine. The Sleezers have already spent the down payment within minutes of announcing the sale."

"We haven't taken bids or explored alternatives to relocation." Straus smiled his smarmy smile. Ethan was certain the man was posturing. Everyone in this room knew the team was Ethan's.

"The time to do that is long past," Cyrus spoke up. "I expect you to honor the original agreement we made or be prepared for a nasty lawsuit this league has never seen the likes of before."

The commissioner blanched. "There's no need for legal action."

"You're right, there isn't," Ethan said. "Even if other interested parties come up with the funds to buy this team at the current price, you're well aware I'm willing to raise their offer by one-hundred million."

"They can't," Straus admitted, as he wiped sweat off his forehead. "The team is yours." Straus had given up too soon, proving to Ethan he'd never truly taken the other offer seriously, even though he'd played both sides.

"Thank you. I'd say this conversation is over and done." Ethan didn't care for Straus and the less time spent in his company the better.

"Actually, it isn't. Not yet. Cooper Black is waiting outside to discuss this situation. You might as well hear what he has to say."

Ethan suppressed his surprise. Straus had scheduled back-to-back meetings with Cooper and Ethan for a reason, either to wield his power over both men or to prove some unforeseen point. Standing, Straus opened the door. A very angry Cooper stalked into the room. He looked ready to start a brawl any second. As if he'd already known they'd be there, he barely glanced at the other men and focused his attention on Straus, who'd returned to his seat.

"I'm not going to Seattle, and the league needs to prevent this move," Cooper said, getting to the point.

Ethan said nothing. He'd done this to Cooper and his entire

time. Cooper didn't trust easily. Ethan had earned his trust then smashed it to pieces like a rare vase meeting its destiny on a concrete sidewalk. He'd shattered something too fragile to put back together, but business was business, and hockey was not just a passion, it was a business. Not just for Ethan, but for Cooper. Despite his anger and the negative emotions surrounding the team's move, Cooper was a Sockeye, like it or not.

"I've read your request. While it's heartfelt and you have my sympathies and understanding, the team is moving." The commissioner sat back in his huge chair and sighed. "You don't get a vote in this. Your only other choice is to sit out next season."

Cooper shot an angry glare at Ethan, obviously blaming him for this power play. "You wouldn't do that." He addressed Straus.

"I would. Try me." The commissioner showed some major cajones to cross Cooper Black like that.

Cooper's eyes narrowed. He flicked his gaze to Ethan, who stayed out of the conversation. "Fine. I'll go to Seattle, but I'm not liking it one bit. I always leave my blood and guts out on the ice, and that won't change, but don't expect anything off the ice."

"I'm paying you to win hockey games. Those are my expectations." Ethan raised an eyebrow, playing the part of the badass owner, even as it ripped him to shreds over the damage he'd done to Cooper, a man he held in the highest regard.

Cooper's eyes narrowed to slits of ice-blue fire. "You have my word as a professional. That's more than I can say for you."

Ethan didn't defend his actions. They weren't exactly defensible. "That's all I can ask."

Cooper cast one more murderous glare at Ethan and the commissioner and walked from the room. The door clicked shut softly behind him, which said more than any slamming door ever would.

* * * *

Seattle.

Land of rain and gray skies.

But right now it wasn't gray or raining. It was a gloriously sunny June day in the seventies, showcasing snow-capped mountains, blue water, and vibrant green hills. Green everywhere as far as Lauren could see. She'd never seen so much green in her life. Ever. An abundance of trees hid the homes on the hills, giving the distinct impression that except for the downtown area and the horrendous traffic, no one lived here.

But they did.

Seattle was a large metropolitan area and had the snarling traffic to prove it.

There really were Starbucks on every corner, and people dressed like function took precedence over fashion. She'd read an article once naming Seattle as the worst dressed city in the nation. Now she believed it.

Despite the glaring beauty, she refused to fall prey to the city's charms. The trees and mountains made her claustrophobic. The traffic rendered travel during any time but the dead of night more frustrating than trying to get Brick to put on some clothes. Housing prices were so outrageous, even with her generous raise, she didn't think she could afford anything more than a cardboard box under the Alaskan Way Viaduct.

Lauren settled Horace into their large apartment overlooking Lake Union, courtesy of the Sockeyes. He'd made the trip with her after his family moved out of her old apartment building and left him homeless. Convinced Horace was as happy as any grouchy cat could be, she headed to the team's temporary headquarters near the old arena at Seattle City Center, the team's home away from home until the new arena was completed a few blocks away.

Half the staff didn't make the trip, but Ethan gave them generous severance packages; even Lauren had to admit being impressed. He'd done everything he could to make the transition as smooth as possible for the remaining staff. Unfortunately, except for Kaley, the remaining staff avoided her as if she were to blame for their situation. In some ways, she did feel responsible, considering the insider intel she'd shared with Ethan.

Her father hadn't spoken to her since an accusing conversation the day after the announcement. She didn't believe he'd actually quit the team yet. She'd heard Ethan offered him an embarrassing amount of money to stay on until they could replace him.

The new coaching staff had been hired only a few days after the *takeover*, as she'd come to think of the situation. The new coach had been an assistant coach on three championship teams. Lauren knew of him. He was young, fiery, and progressive. Everything Ethan wanted in a coach, and so was his staff. The new GM was also young and innovative. This group didn't do anything by the book, and under any other circumstances, Lauren would be giddy with excitement over the positive changes.

But she wasn't. She'd slept with her boss, she'd compromised her friends' trust, many of whom had been let go or quit, and she'd alienated her family. Even her brothers avoided her. Aunt Jo on the other hand, laughed at the men in the family, declaring they were pouting like two-year-olds with their training pants in a twist.

Lauren dreaded this first official meeting of the Sockeyes' staff, hoping Ethan would be doing whatever billionaires did to earn more billions. Afterward she had appointments to meet with the GM and new director of player personnel, her direct boss. She worried herself sick about making a good impression. Even if she wasn't staying with the team after her contract period, she'd need their recommendations to land another job in the league or even with a minor league team.

With views of the Space Needle and the water, the Sockeyes building was an old brick structure which had been remodeled recently without losing its 1900s charm. Charming or not, a building was just a building. It was what was inside that counted.

Entering the conference room, Lauren was the first one there. She took a seat near the middle of the long table and waited.

Ten minutes later, the new general manager, Garrett Calhoun, walked in. The man was known for his brilliant moves regarding draft choices and team personnel. He took a seat next to head coach Mike Gorst. On Gorst's other side sat Lars Ericksen, Lauren's new boss and the director of player personnel.

Lauren looked away. A few others trickled in. The familiar faces avoided eye contact with her, while the new faces smiled eagerly. Lauren was happy to see a few women in the group. Kaley took a seat next to Lauren, while Mina, Ethan's formidable administrative assistant pulled out an iPad, and started taking notes. The ancient woman's fingers danced across the screen with the dexterity of a teenager.

Lauren fidgeted. The one person she dreaded seeing would walk through that door any minute, and the group didn't wait long. Flanked by Brad, Ethan strode into the room with an air of authority no one could miss. Several others followed him and took their seats.

Lauren hadn't seen him in two weeks. At the sight of the man, her fickle heart did flips that would do a circus tumbling act proud.

Ethan smiled at her. Still not dressed in a suit—none of the assembled staff were—he wore a blue Sockeyes T-shirt with a logo of a lime green fish with a black eye holding a hockey stick. Since when were fish lime green?

Ethan introduced his management team, as he called it, and his investors, including Brad Reynolds, members of Reynolds' family and Ethan's family.

It was all very formal, and luckily short and to the point. She expected no less from Ethan—a man of action and not many words, unlike the Sleezers who would drone on forever until Lauren wanted to poke her eyes out with her pen.

After the brief introductions, a statement of purpose, and some rah-rah on how they were going to build a perpetual winner, Ethan, Brad, and the investors excused themselves, while the group broke up into smaller group meetings.

As Ethan walked by her chair their eyes met. He nodded briefly at her. Lauren looked away, gripping the edge of the table, as if her racing heart might force her feet to sprint out the door after him.

She let out a breath and glanced around the room, hoping no one noticed her reaction to Ethan. She didn't want the new staff to believe she'd slept her way into a position with the Sockeyes, even if the handful of staff who'd moved with the team already thought that. She'd gotten this job on her own merits, and she'd damn well prove her qualifications to every person in this room.

She may not want to be in Seattle, but she'd do her job to the best of her ability.

* * * *

A week later, Kaley watched Lauren over the rim of her wine glass, but made no comment. Obviously, she noticed how quiet Lauren had been all day long.

"So your Aunt Jo is moving to Seattle?"

"I tried to talk her out of it. I'm not staying here."

"Living here is turning into a regular family affair." A note of sadness entered Kaley's usual sassy voice. Kaley never talked about her family, and Lauren discovered early in their friendship to never ask. It was a huge sore spot with her friend.

"I'd hardly say that. Just my aunt. She's been wanting a change and loves this city, always wanted to live here. Go figure."

Kaley nodded. "I'm loving it, too." She waved her arms, hitting a waiter in the process. Kaley giggled and batted her eyes at the guy, and Lauren could tell he'd follow her anywhere. "What's not to love? Look at this view. You don't get a view like this very many places on earth."

Lauren stared out the window of the waterfront restaurant at Puget Sound and the Olympic Mountains in the distance. She couldn't dispute the beauty, especially on sunny days, but she still didn't want to be here working side-by-side with Ethan, a constant reminder of what a stupid fool she'd been once again. Some women never learned. Max ripped out her heart, but Ethan not only ripped it out, he stomped it into a bloody pulp and left it for dead.

"What's up with your father?"

"I don't know. He's not talking to me, and I'm not asking Ethan. I don't have a clue if he quit or what, but I did hear Ethan made him an offer he'd be nuts to refuse."

"As a scout, he doesn't have to live here."

Lauren nodded and sighed. "I know. So does he. Ethan has big plans for this team, but I doubt Dad wants any part of this team."

"And you? You still don't want to be a part of what he's building here?" Lauren had walked into that one, foolish as she'd been.

"You know what hurts the most? He didn't trust me enough to confide in me. He kept me in the dark along with everyone else."

"Maybe he couldn't tell you. Maybe he didn't have a choice."

"Maybe he should've trusted me enough to know that I would've kept his secret."

"How would you have handled it even if you'd known?"

"Not well," Lauren admitted.

"There you go. He was damned if he did, damned if he didn't."

"He convinced me to sign an employment contract under false pretenses."

"Okay, I admit that was a little shitty, but everything I've heard about Ethan since being in this town indicates his family is held in the highest regard. They give back, actively participate in community functions, and have great reputations as being progressive and caring employers."

Lauren knew all that. She'd done her own research. The Parker family had been in Seattle since the early days and built their fortunes on hard work, ethical practices, and honest dealings. They were incredible community leaders and generous to those who earned their respect. All in all, too good to be true.

"He's made some great decisions regarding staff and coaches. I've been impressed so far."

Lauren had been, too. Ethan had hired a young, passionate staff full of progressive, somewhat controversial ideas and methods. The new coaches and GM spent hours poring over film and asking her questions about the current roster, who to keep, what to change, and what kind of talent might be available for the right price. She'd been taken aback when they'd first invited her to join them and actually listened to her opinions, sharing their own, and essentially treating her as an equal. They'd studied her advanced stats and taken mounds of notes.

Ethan had filled the team's front offices with the best and brightest, sparing no expense, and the league had taken notice. It was even rumored a couple prize free agents were making it known they'd entertain offers from Seattle. They wouldn't have looked twice at the team under the previous management. Lauren wished she could discuss the changes with her father, get his take on it, but so far the man remained off her radar, and her brothers refused to share any insights with her.

Kaley snapped her fingers in front of Lauren's face. "Hey, you still here?"

"Sorry. I was thinking about all the changes. I have to admit he's made some good ones."

Kaley's eyes grew big. "There's hope for you yet, girl."

Lauren rolled her eyes. "Not where Ethan is concerned, at least not on a personal level."

"But? I hear a but."

"I enjoy working with the new staff."

"Admit it. You want to stay."

"I can't work with Ethan." All this talk about Ethan tied her stomach in knots and left her feeling confused and uncertain. "How's it going with Brad?" Lauren flipped the conversation to

Kaley.

Hurt flashed in her friend's eyes. "Oh, we aren't seeing each other except as friends. Maybe later, but right now he's juggling a lot of balls and I'm getting used to a new city." Kaley wasn't telling her everything but Lauren decided to let it drop for now.

"Know what you need?" Kaley continued. "New town. New you. You need a makeover. I've been considering one myself. Let's go together."

Lauren started to say no, then decided why the hell not?

She was a new Lauren in a new city with essentially a new team. And this new Lauren could stand to spruce up her appearance. After all she had the money now, but did she have the guts?

Yes, she did.

* * * *

Ethan saw Lauren in passing and in meetings over the next few weeks, and he let well enough alone, even though it killed him to do so. He couldn't sleep, despite working out to the point of exhaustion every evening like a crazed man. He poured himself into the job, trying to forget her, but how do you forget a woman like her? Especially when her office was on the same floor as his. They attended many of the same meetings, and he'd completely space out, not hearing a word the speaker said, as he stared at her beautiful face when she wasn't looking. He was a mess, and he had to pull himself together. He had a team to run, but even his passion for hockey hadn't driven his passion for her from his thoughts or his fantasies.

Tonight, he left the Sockeye offices as the setting sun burst into brilliant reds, oranges, and blues across the smooth-as-glass water. For some weird reason, the sunset reminded him of Lauren. It wasn't like they'd shared sunset walks together, but everything reminded him of Lauren in some obscure way.

He was halfway to his car when he noticed the current occupier of his thoughts standing at the bus stop. He detoured over to her. "Something happen to your car?"

She jumped, as if he'd frightened her. "Don't ever sneak up on me again."

"Sorry, didn't mean to scare you." He took in her new look and stared harder. She'd put blonde streaks in her light brown hair and the cute little dress she wore was definitely new and damn sexy. He suppressed the urge to wolf-whistle, knowing how tacky and inappropriate it'd be given their current situation.

"My car is in the shop," she explained, fidgeting with her purse. He suspected if she'd smoked, she'd be lighting one up right about now, and he'd be joining her.

"Could I give you a ride home? The bus doesn't come for another hour or so."

"It doesn't?" She glanced down the street, as if not believing him.

"I don't know," he admitted. He hadn't a clue about the bus schedule. He followed her gaze down the street, silently hoping the bus didn't come trundling around the corner any second.

"Being alone with you is not a good idea."

Right now he thought it was the best damn idea ever. "Lauren, it's getting dark. This isn't a bad neighborhood, but still, it's not wise for a lone woman to be waiting for the bus. I'd feel responsible if something happened."

She hesitated, and he could almost hear her arguing with herself. Finally, she sighed. "All right," she said reluctantly, obviously not interested in getting any closer to him than required by the job.

Ethan didn't blame her, but he desperately missed the conversations they'd once shared. He'd love to hear her take on his staff changes, whether or not she approved, and if she had a gauge on the players' reactions to their new environment, or had ideas for under-the-radar free agents they should pursue.

Why not pick her brain? She was on his payroll. Like many of his decisions, he made a split second one. "Lauren, I'd like to talk to you, hear your take on how things are going. I'd be grateful if you'd let me drive you home, maybe get a burger and talk about our mutual passion."

Her eyes grew big, and he chuckled. "Hockey, Lauren, hockey."

"You're incorrigible." Her eyes narrowed and her face took on an attractive shade of red he enjoyed so much. Thank God the old Lauren still existed under her shiny, new exterior because this Lauren unnerved him a little.

"So? It's a deal, right?" He sounded pathetically hopeful, even to his own ears.

She made a show of trying to decide, but he knew her well

enough to recognize the signs. Lauren couldn't resist talking hockey even with her Enemy Number One—him. "Okay, but just a hamburger and one beer, then I have to go to bed." At his quick glance, she added, "By myself." She quirked a brow at him.

He chuckled, feeling a pound or two of the heavy weight of guilt lift off his shoulders. "You drive a hard bargain."

"Always."

"That's one of the things I like about you."

She smiled coyly, one of those sexy old movie siren smiles like her namesake, and his heart picked up its pace, thumping against his ribcage in the same fast rhythm as the beat of a classic Bon Jovi song. Oh, yeah, she'd shot him through the heart all right.

"So, please. Join me."

She nodded once, playing it cool. He didn't mind. He deserved cool after how he'd deceived her even if he hadn't been given an option.

They walked to the car together, and he opened the door for her, almost groaning when her dress rode up and gave him a good eyeful of her shapely thigh. He crossed to his side, slowing down behind the car to gather his composure, but the only thing he gathered was an aching hard-on.

Ethan drove to a small café near the water. The neon closed sign blinked blue and pink. "I guess we're too late. I'll find somewhere else."

She turned toward him, and her purse slipped off her lap. He leaned down to pick it up off the floor at the same time she did. They both froze. Their lips were inches apart. Lauren's eyes dilated turning a deep green, and her lips parted, while Ethan's common sense skated for the penalty box. He didn't know who made the next move. Maybe they both did. A split second later, they were kissing the hell out of each other, completely out of control and roughly wild. It'd been too long since his tongue and hers danced together, and he took full advantage of her compliance, deepening his kiss.

Lauren pulled back first, her palms flattened against his chest. With great reluctance, he released her, panting and seriously attempting to regain some semblance of normalcy.

He ran his hands over his face. "I'm sorry, Lauren. That shouldn't have happened."

"But it did. Let's forget it and move on." Her breathy voice betrayed how little she'd moved on despite her brave words.

"I suppose dinner is out of the question right now?"

"Yes." She avoided his gaze.

Ethan nodded grimly, asked for her address, and drove her home in total silence except for the sound of their harsh breathing. He walked her to her door, made sure she got inside safely, and told her good night, knowing it wouldn't be a good night for him, and he doubted it would be for her either.

Just when he'd been making a little progress, he'd fucked up by letting his emotions override his professionalism once again and pushing her further than she was ready to go.

Ethan hated the thought of losing her and not just as an employee. He'd hoped she'd come around after more time passed, and he didn't know how much longer he could wait. He'd proven he couldn't keep his hands and mouth off her.

He'd been using the contract to force her to stay. What if he offered to release her from her contract in a goodwill gesture with the hope she'd realize she didn't want to leave.

He'd be taking a huge gamble, which would force her hand. He wasn't certain he was ready to let go if she accepted his offer.

Chapter 15—Rebound

A few days later, the newly christened Seattle Sockeyes hosted their first ever fan appreciation day. Kaley and Mina had put their heads together and planned an all-day affair at a nearby rink including beginning classes on how to watch hockey, basic hockey rules, and a player meet-and-greet autograph session.

Lauren volunteered to help and couldn't believe the turnout. The six-thousand person arena was filled to the max long before the players skated onto the ice for introductions. Not all the players made the trip to Seattle for this first appearance, but Cooper and Cedric's agents twisted their arms, and the guys showed up. Despite Cooper's dislike of all things Sockeye, he was a hit with the fans and treated them respectfully and graciously. Ethan made a cameo appearance, gave a short speech about hockey in Seattle, then faded into the background. Lauren bustled around, making sure things ran smoothly, and following Mina's barked orders. No one crossed Mina when she was in Sergeant-Major mode, not even Ethan.

At the end of the long exhausting day, Lauren dragged her tired body to headquarters to finish some reports on free agents for the GM. She hesitated when she spotted Cedric and Cooper, along with a few other players loitering near the players' lounge.

Steeling herself for the cold shoulder from Cooper, she continued her approach, head held high and a friendly smile pasted on her face. "Hello, gentlemen. Good to see you guys."

Cedric grinned at her, ever the charmer. "You're looking good, Lauren."

Cooper just grunted and ignored her. After all, she was the enemy now.

"Can you believe the turnout? The enthusiasm? The fan support blew me away. I've never seen anything like it. We sold out of T-shirts, banners, just about everything." Only having the former Giants as a measuring stick, Lauren never imagined in her wildest dreams the Sockeyes would garner such fan support before they skated in one game.

Cooper scowled and opened his mouth to say something, but Cedric jumped in with a reply. "Yeah, they loved seeing the Beauty and the Beast. I'm the beauty, and he's the beast." He pointed at his chest then at Cooper's. Cedric grinned at his buddy and slapped him on the back.

Cooper just grunted as he stared at the logo on the T-shirt Cedric wore. "What the hell is Sockeye anyway?"

"It's a salmon, Coop. Don't be a dumbshit. Get with the program." Cedric got a chuckle out of needling Cooper, who didn't look the least bit amused.

"Salmon? Who names a hockey team after a salmon?" Cooper made a face. "What a stupid logo. A fish with a black eye holding a hockey stick. You have to be kidding me."

Cedric just grinned all the more and turned to Lauren. "Coop loves the new uni's."

"Like hell. The only fish I want to see on ice is the fresh one I just caught for dinner."

"Don't you love his positive outlook?" Cedric didn't let Cooper off the hook.

"You might work on your attitude a little there, Coop," Lauren agreed.

Cooper narrowed his eyes and glared at her. "This coming from someone who sold out her colleagues and friends to get ahead in this organization?"

"I didn't do that. I—" Okay so maybe it did look like that. A lot of Ethan's personnel decisions had been based in part on her input.

"You did, Lauren. You screwed over the staff, just like you screwed Ethan. Only the staff didn't find it nearly as enjoyable." Cooper stared down at her, his blue eyes blazing with pent-up frustration and anger.

"That's enough. Apologize to the lady." Ethan stepped up to Lauren's side. With his clenched fists and ice-blue eyes, he looked ready to take on Cooper and the entire damn hockey team.

Cooper's smirk indicated he'd welcome a fist fight with Ethan if Ethan would be kind enough to oblige. Ethan didn't back down, and Lauren stepped in the middle of two angry alpha males. Cedric stood nearby, ready to assist, and she appreciated his calm presence.

"I said, apologize to the lady. You're on my payroll, and you'll treat my staff with respect."

A muscle ticked in Cooper's jaw and for one tense moment Lauren feared the situation might escalate out of control. Finally Coop let out a breath and turned to her. "Sorry, Lauren. I was out of line."

"That's okay." She managed a weak smile.

Cooper turned to Cedric. "I need a beer." Cooper stalked down the hall followed by his small group of teammates. A few of the young guys glanced nervously over their shoulders. They needed their jobs. Cooper didn't.

Lauren waited until they rounded a corner. "Thanks for defending me, but I can handle myself with these guys. In fact, in order to gain back their respect, I insist on handling them myself in the future."

Ethan's eyes softened, and he smiled sadly at her. "I understand, but I need to establish boundaries as to the treatment of my staff."

Lauren sighed. *His* staff. Another reminder she was part of his staff and would be until she could fulfill her contract and get the hell out of this city and away from this man whose body tempted her to throw away everything just for another fling with him.

Ethan cleared his throat. "I was wondering if you'd meet me for dinner. Strictly business, of course."

Unwelcome excitement flooded through her. She wanted to meet him, but not for business. Regardless, business was better than nothing. "I can spare some time."

As if she hadn't learned her lesson the last time. When it came to Ethan, she suspected she'd never learn that particular lesson.

* * * *

Minutes later, Lauren sat across from Ethan in a booth at a neighborhood bar called simply The Place which he claimed served some of the best burgers in Seattle. She longed for the days when there hadn't been this awkward silence between them, and they talked hockey and made love into all hours of the night.

A wire-thin waitress as rough as the cracked and worn menus she carried hustled up to their table. Her all-business, take-no-prisoners expression softened when she recognized Ethan. A huge smile spread across her face.

"Ethan, about time you came in. Been cooling your heels in the ice rink watching your new team?" she asked as she tossed the menus on the table and tapped her pencil against her pad. Her makeup hid whether she was a worn-out forty or twice that age.

Judging by her hands, Lauren voted for the latter.

"Team doesn't report to training camp for a while. You a hockey fan, Doris?" Ethan chatted her up, obviously knowing her. This didn't seem like the type of place a billionaire would frequent, but Ethan wasn't your typical billionaire, preferring jeans to suits and ties, and never talking down to those in lower financial brackets. Lauren grudgingly admitted he had lots of good qualities. Too bad honesty wasn't among them. And too bad forgiveness wasn't among hers.

"I am now. The rainy season has been long and empty since the Sonics left, and I like a good fight as much as the next girl." Lauren suspected Doris had been in a few fights herself over the years.

"I'll send you some tickets, right down on the glass."

"I'll hold you to it. Sorry I missed your big day today. I heard about it from several fans who came in afterward." The waitress walked off toward a bar where an even crustier, tattooed bartender with a bald head and a beefy body made drinks.

"That was nice of you." The words tumbled out before she could stop them. After all, dishing out compliments to the man who had uprooted her life and the lives of many of her friends and colleagues wasn't on her to-do list.

"I'm a nice guy." He grinned that engaging grin of his, and she almost fell for it once again.

Lauren cocked her head and spiked a brow, duly disputing his claim with just one eyebrow. "She's a character."

"A Seattle institution, just like this place. It's been here for as long as I can remember and so has she. Not much changes except the photos." He pointed to the walls lined with autographs of what appeared to be local Seattle sports stars and celebrities. He pointed at a shot of a basketball team dressed in green and gold. "That's the 1979 Sonics championship team, may they rest in peace. There's the 1917 Seattle Metropolitans—the first American team to win the Cup."

Lauren nodded. She'd known that about Seattle.

Ethan turned to her, his enthusiasm bubbling over in that way she'd always admired. "Years from now I want to walk into this place with my grandkids and point at a picture of the Seattle Sockeyes hoisting the Cup on home ice and say this was the first Sockeye team to win the Cup."

"That's quite a dream." Lauren smiled at him, feeling as if she'd come to understand him a little bit more with his simple story. Given the same circumstances, she wondered if she'd poach another city's hockey team, despite the consequences, and move it to a city like Seattle.

Sadness washed over her. She wouldn't be a part of what he was building. She'd be walking away from the Sockeyes as soon as legally possible.

"What can I say? I dream big. What's the point of dreaming small?" His blue eyes shone with pride.

But Ethan wasn't just a dreamer. He made his dreams reality, and he had the money to do it.

Lauren studied his expression, trying to read his thoughts, his hopes, his fears. If only he'd trusted her with his secret. There was only one way to find out and damned if she had the guts to ask tough questions with answers she might not appreciate.

"You're staring. Did I say something wrong?" His smile dropped a few notches.

"Uh, no. Not at all."

"Good, I'd rather not piss you off any more than I already have."

There it was. He'd opened the door a crack. She could kick it open the rest of the way and let all kinds of uncomfortable things inside or she could slam it shut and lock it.

"You didn't piss me off. You disappointed me, more than you'll ever know."

"I'm sorry for that." He looked genuinely sorry. In fact, his sadness knocked on the door to her heart.

Lauren wavered but shored up her resolve to keep this meal strictly on a business level, not that there was anything to waver over. After all, except for one slip, Ethan hadn't made one move to re-establish anything other than a purely business relationship.

"You invited me here with the promise of discussing business. So let's discuss hockey, or you can take me home." Harsh words, but she couldn't give the man an inch, because her heart would gladly give him a mile.

"You're right." He sat back and took a sip of beer then sighed. "Have you heard anything from your father?"

"Nothing."

"That makes two of us. I told him to take a few weeks to make a decision."

"I'm sure he'll get back to you. If for no other reason than to tell you where to shove your offer."

Ethan laughed. "I'm sure you're right." He leaned forward and sobered a little. "How are things going for you? Are the new coaches treating you well?"

Lauren couldn't stop her smile. "Really well." She couldn't lie. She adored the new coaches, loved their enthusiasm, dedication, and open-minded attitudes.

"They're listening to you?" His anxious expression indicated how much her answer mattered.

"Yes. A lot."

"Good. I've heard great things about you, too, from them. They tell me you have an eye for hockey talent, for numbers, and analyzing what those numbers actually mean. All stuff I'd already known."

"I'm happy to be able to help." She spoke with absolute sincerity.

"Are you enjoying your new role? I sure as hell hope you are because you're invaluable to me and this team."

His blue eyes held her captive, and her heart performed those familiar back flips it did whenever she looked into those mesmerizing eyes of his. Lauren looked away, tamping down her over-enthusiastic heart. Ethan's approval was invaluable to her and so was Ethan. She wished it wasn't that way, but there it was.

He sat back in the booth and ran a hand through his still unruly hair. He'd shaved but hadn't bothered to cut his hair in a while. Most likely he got so busy, he didn't get around to it.

"If you want out, Lauren, I'll void the contract. You keep the money. The only thing I ask of you is to stay through the draft to assist the coaching staff."

A huge lump prevented Lauren from answering. She couldn't continue as Ethan's employee when she wanted so much more. Being his lover wouldn't be enough for her, her pride, or her sense of professionalism. Nor would it earn her the respect of the staff, players, and coaches. She was in a lose-lose situation. The only way to cut her losses to a minimum was to leave.

"I think it's for the best if I go." Her voice cracked on that last word.

"All right, then. I'll start looking for your replacement. If you have any ideas, let me know." Ethan's face hardened into a mask of neutrality.

"I will. I'm not really hungry. Could you please take me home now?"

Ethan threw an ample amount of cash on the table and drove her home in silence. He waited while she went inside and locked the door behind her.

Lauren peered through the blinds, watching him walk to his car with his shoulders slumped, every stride announcing defeat. A minute later she heard his car drive off.

She slumped to the floor, her back against the door. Horace rubbed up against her, purring loudly. She buried her head in her hands and sobbed, crying for what couldn't be, crying for what she'd lost before she'd ever gained it, and most of all crying for losing Ethan.

* * * *

Ethan hated it when his requests were ignored, especially by his own staff. He paid people to handle the details so he didn't have to sweat the small stuff and could focus on the big picture. It was so atypical for Mina to let crap go like this. He stomped over to her desk feeling every bit like a grouchy grizzly bear. Mina ignored him as she went over a marketing plan with Brad, making Ethan wait. Finally, she glanced up at him and cocked one eyebrow. Brad stood back and watched with way too much interest.

"Mina, I told you I don't want anyone scheduled during this time frame. Why the hell did you schedule a Seattle Times interview?"

"Because you said it's crucial we promote the hell out of the team. They want to do a feature and that was the only time I could squeeze them in."

Ethan continued to glower at her; he couldn't help it. He was in that kind of mood. "Don't do it again without asking me first."

"Yes, my king." Mina answered in mock seriousness, and Brad snorted with laughter.

Damn, he got no respect from the old bat, but firing her wasn't an option. He didn't have a clue how he'd function without her. Brad followed him into his office, even though he tried to close the door on his friend. He wasn't in the mood for company. That'd never stopped Brad.

His buddy helped himself to a cup of fresh coffee from the Keurig machine and sprawled on the leather couch, feet on the glass coffee table.

"I have work to do, and I bet you do, too." Ethan spoke pointedly. Ethan had been surprisingly impressed at how hard Brad worked on marketing the team. Of course, Brad had been gifted with a silver tongue so selling hockey to Seattle ran right up his alley.

"Yeah, and you've been a regular asshole lately. Everyone's noticed."

"You mean more than usual?"

"Come on, Ethan. You're not an asshole to work with. In fact, you're usually a pretty damn good guy, so what's up with you?"

Ethan frowned. He hadn't realized he'd been coming across as an ass to his employees. "I—I'm not sure." He couldn't be more honest than that.

"It's got to be a woman. Did you and Lauren settle your differences?" Brad's eyes narrowed as he studied his friend, dissecting his body language like no one else could.

"You could say we did."

"Oh, shit, you're not sleeping with her again? You can't be, or you'd be in a better mood." Brad answered his own question.

Ethan sighed. Sometimes Brad was a bigger pain in the ass than Mina. "I let her out of her contract. She'll be leaving after the draft."

"Are you fucking kidding me? The draft is next week. She's a crucial part of our staff. Why did you do a stupid-assed thing like that?" Brad narrowed his eyes and glared at Ethan.

"She's a brilliant hockey mind, but she wanted out. I'm not going to force anyone to stay. I know the team is going to suffer for it. I hate to see her go." Ethan rubbed his face with his hands, suddenly wearier than he'd been in days.

"That's not the only reason you hate to see her go. You're hot for her."

Ethan shrugged. He couldn't reduce what he and Lauren had together down to hockey and sex. It just cheapened a relationship which had stood for so much more.

Brad studied him in that way only Brad could, passing judgment without opening his mouth.

"What?" Ethan said.

"Well, I guess it's better for both of you. While having a fling with her might put a dent in your reputation, it'd ruin hers and her ability to be taken seriously ever again."

"I know. I never thought I'd be running this hockey team without her practical and sound advice."

Brad nodded. "I think you two had a good partnership going. If you don't want to let her go, and you want a personal relationship, there is an option, though somewhat drastic."

"An option? What the hell would that be?" Ethan would gladly take a drastic option over losing Lauren any day.

"Propose."

"Propose what?"

"Since when are you so dense? Marry the woman. She can still work for the organization without repercussions, and you two can have endless booty calls."

"They don't call them booty calls when you're married."

"What would I know about that?"

"So you're saying have my cake and eat it too by marrying her?" Ethan seriously wondered if Brad had been partaking in some of Seattle's now-legal emerald weed.

"Yeah, it's perfect." Brad grinned, as if he'd just solved all Ethan's problems.

"That's nuts. Propose marriage to keep her here?" And in his bed? Even more importantly, in his life?

"Hey, my parents got married with less in common than that, and it turned out okay."

"Yeah, but they had some rocky times."

"Who doesn't? They're still together and happier than they've ever been. And look at your parents. They're so happy together, they're damn disgusting. You've had good role models. Why couldn't you make it work?"

"What about love, Brad? The reason most people marry."

"Yeah, and get divorced six months later. Highly overrated, I say."

"You've been holding out on me. I've never seen your cynical side."

Brad snorted. "You'll never catch me getting married for love. It's an illusion. I'll get married because it makes good business sense, to have kids, and because we're compatible enough not to kill each other when I leave my underwear on the floor or she spreads her makeup all over the bathroom counter."

Ethan just shook his head. "You, my man, have a major issue."

"Like you don't?"

"You're the one telling me to put a ring on her finger to keep her here." Ethan pointed out the obvious but Brad just grinned. "Like I said, you're nuts. Not going to happen. It's one of your stupider ideas."

Brad's sly smile indicated he knew something Ethan didn't. "Someday you'll be eating those words and I'll be feasting on your apology."

Brad had pickled his brain from all the partying he'd done in college. That was the only thing that could explain his insane suggestion.

Marry Lauren just to keep her here? That would be absolute insanity.

And Ethan had always been stone-cold sober when it came to sanity, though he did have a penchant for following his gut.

Even after Brad left the office, Ethan couldn't drive the idea out of his head. Maybe it was time to get drunk on insanity and do an incredibly insane thing.

Lauren, he realized, was worth a bout of insanity, or so his gut told him.

Chapter 16—Tripping

Lauren resisted the urge to chew her fingernails as she sat with Kaley in a small cafe after a late night at work. Everyone worked long hours getting ready for free agency and the draft. Kaley and Lauren were no exception. Kaley's new responsibilities revolved around assisting with the salary cap and prospective player research, and she excelled in her new role with the team. A role Lauren grudgingly admitted Kaley would never have had with the former management.

"Ethan's doing incredible things with this team," Kaley gushed, as if she'd been promoted to the president of the Ethan Parker Fan Club.

"Yes, he is. His methods are cutting edge and not exactly making him friends with the good ol' boys, but he's heading in the right direction."

"You do?" One perfectly sculpted eyebrow peaked under Kaley's brow. "Then you're staying?"

The urge to jump up and shout, *hell, yes, I want to be part of this thing he's building here even if I have to tolerate months of rain,* reverberated through her. It took every ounce of willpower she possessed to stick with her plan, even if she didn't have a clue what her plan might entail. "Actually, the opposite. He released me from my contract. I can leave right after the draft."

"But your aunt just moved here."

"She didn't move here to be with me. She moved here because she believes Seattle is a beautiful, progressive city, and she's always wanted to live here. Me being here gave her that needed kick in the ass."

"But she still moved because you're here."

Lauren sighed, feeling cranky and defensive. "She'll stay here because she wants to, and my decision to go has nothing to do with her."

"Why did he let you out of your contract? Something happened, didn't it?" Kaley rubbed her chin in thought. "I honestly thought the last few weeks would convince you to stay."

Lauren squeezed her eyes shut, not wanting to answer her best friend's question. She answered it anyway. "I can't work with him on a professional level without the personal entering into it. I just can't. The man attracts me too much."

"So?"

"So, I work for him. All the respect I fought to earn over the past several years is blown to pieces by a sexual relationship with him. I didn't get this job because I slept with him, I got it because I'm damn good at evaluating hockey talent even if I don't have a penis."

"You are, and this staff knows that. They listen. Where are you going to find a progressive organization like this that values your opinion?"

"Lots of teams."

"Those teams don't have openings, and most of all, they don't have Ethan."

"That's the point. They don't have Ethan. If I have to take less money with a minor league team and work my way back up, I'll do it."

Kaley blew out one of those long-suffering sighs. "Call me selfish, but I'll miss you. What'll I do without my partner in crime?"

"I'm hardly your partner in crime. More like your voice of reason."

"Still, I've dragged you down some naughty paths a few times."

Nothing like the ones Ethan had dragged her down.

Not anymore.

She'd walk away with her head held high and never look back. Even if it was the greenest place she'd ever lived. With the bluest water. And the most gorgeous mountains. And the handsomest, most infuriating billionaire.

Damn it all to hell. In a short time, Seattle had soaked into her skin just like Ethan had soaked into her heart.

She didn't want to leave either one of them.

SKATING ON THIN ICE (SEATTLE SOCKEYES)—GAME ON IN SEATTLE 1

Chapter 17—High Stick

After the last player in the draft was selected, the staff threw an office party. Lauren tried to sneak out, but Kaley cornered her and herded her back inside. None of the other staff realized this was her last day. She hated goodbyes, and she'd set up a deferred email to be sent out tomorrow.

She sipped a glass of wine and mingled, a word here, a word there. When she heard Mina talking to another of Ethan's long-time employees and heard his name, she was all ears. What she heard should've surprised her, yet it made perfect sense. Ethan had been burned before by having a personal relationship with a former female employee. She'd sued him. They settled out of court for a large sum, and Ethan had sworn never again. Until her. No wonder he decided to release her from her contract. The generous offer hadn't been for her sake but for his, and she'd misinterpreted a man's motives once again.

Still processing what she'd heard, she hoped to make it through the party without seeing Ethan, who had been conspicuously absent all evening. Even though they'd agreed to her leaving after the draft, she doubted he realized she'd be walking out of Sockeye headquarters—lovingly christened the Fish Bowl by Mina—for the last time that evening.

Unfortunately, her fast getaway wasn't to be. Beer already in hand, Ethan strolled in and spotted her immediately. Now she knew how a deer felt when it looked into the headlights of an oncoming car. She wanted to bolt but didn't dare. Instead she held her ground and met her fate.

"So how do you think we did?" he asked conversationally.

"In the draft?"

He looked at her kind of funny, as if he didn't get what she meant. "Where else?"

"We did good." Lauren tugged on her Sockeyes T-shirt, suddenly self-conscious of wearing something so blatantly pro-Sockeyes on her last day in the office.

"Nice shirt," Ethan commented. "I love that logo our graphics department designed."

"It's nice."

"The forward you wanted was still there when it came our turn to pick. I'm glad we got him." Ethan shifted from one foot to another, as if being around her made him nervous.

"He flew under the radar." Lauren glanced around, wishing someone would rescue her. No one even looked their way.

"But not under yours."

"You're putting together a good future for this team." Lauren ignored the compliment but couldn't ignore the hunger in Ethan's blue eyes.

"I wish you'd be part of it."

"I can't." She shot down his hopes with those two words.

Ethan sighed. "Will you ever forgive me, Lauren?"

"I don't think I can, Ethan." She whispered her response and met his gaze. Oh, God, what a mistake. His sadness struck deep inside, and pierced her already aching heart. If only— Lauren squelched the thought, as flashbacks of her former husband in bed with three women slammed into her.

Leaving was for the best.

"Then there's no hope for us?" His voice turned husky, laced with regret.

"Ethan, there never was." Her eyes started to fill with tears. She would not cry. Not here. Not in front of the Sockeyes staff, and especially not in front of Ethan.

Ethan nodded, as if understanding even when he didn't. "I thought we made a damn good team together, Lauren."

God, why didn't he just drop this? Another flash of Max flat on his back and focusing his gaze lazily on her as she stood in the doorway holding his birthday cake. He hadn't even cared she'd caught him screwing one woman while the other two attacked the rest of his body. She couldn't get involved deeply with another man. She couldn't take the pain. It hurt enough now, how much would it hurt if she stayed and months down the road he changed his mind?

"Lauren?" Ethan's voice was laced with concern.

"I'm leaving tonight, Ethan. I won't be back. I cleaned out my office and have a message queued to send to staff tomorrow. I didn't announce it because I don't want a fuss."

"I understand." Ethan's expression was unreadable. She couldn't tell how her news affected him, whether he was relieved or sad or nothing at all.

"I hope I'm not putting you in a bind. Have you had any success finding my replacement?"

"I haven't tried. I could never replace you, Lauren." He said it like he meant it. Her throat constricted and she stared down at her feet.

"How about one last dinner talking hockey, the draft, that kind of stuff?"

He dangled the one thing besides sex in front of her she couldn't resist—talking about the game she loved with a man who treated her as an equal.

Lauren should say no, but the sheer need in Ethan's eyes stopped her. One last dinner couldn't hurt. One last memory to hold forever of a very special man who'd nestled in her heart and refused to leave. A man who'd almost made her think she could take a chance on love again until his actions proved to her just why she shouldn't.

Despite it all, she accepted his invitation because it was the last one she'd ever have from him.

* * * *

Ethan waited for Lauren outside a small waterfront restaurant minutes from the Fish Bowl, still surprised she'd said yes, though he shouldn't be, since he'd used hockey for an excuse. Anything to see her again and make one last effort to convince her to stay, not that he had a plan. He'd wing it and pray something brilliant came to mind.

Turning to study the view, he smiled as he gazed around the bustling city and the waterfront with the ferries coming and going, container ships leaving port, and tugboats barging logs. He loved this city. He wished he could teach Lauren to love it, too. In time, he suspected she might, but time was the one thing they didn't have together.

Ethan's week had flown by too fast. The draft was over, a very successful draft from his staff's point of view, and Ethan trusted his staff one-hundred percent. If he didn't, they wouldn't be his staff very long. Despite his euphoria over the draft, a heaviness weighed on his heart. Lauren would be gone unless he launched one last ditch effort to keep her here.

The temptation to do the spontaneous thing, take a leap of faith, and propose had popped into his mind several times a day, even as he batted it down for utter ridiculousness. As ridiculous as the alternative? Life without Lauren? Yeah, but since when did Brad have a good idea, and since when did Ethan listen to his crazy ones?

Once she was gone, he'd get over her. Out of sight, out of mind.

Who was he was kidding? Ethan had always played the game his way, created his own rules within the parameters of his morals and ethics. Only Lauren defied every rule he'd ever made.

He turned as a car came closer. A grin stretched the corners of his mouth as she pulled into the parking spot next to his. His first hockey draft had worn him out but seeing her gave him his second wind, like a much needed shot of adrenaline.

She smiled as she got out of the car, her expression sad yet guarded. Damn, but he knew that feeling. Call him greedy, but he wanted one more night, and he wanted it to last forever.

They lingered over dinner and talked about the draft for two or three hours. Lauren didn't appear to want the night to end any more than Ethan did. He didn't notice they were the last people in the restaurant until the waiter stalked to the table and slapped the bill on it. Apologetic, Ethan paid, and they walked outside to a beautiful, unusually warm night. It was dusk and a brilliant sunset lit up the western skies across the water, illuminating the snow-capped Olympic Mountains in the distance, as if Seattle was pulling out all the stops.

"Let's walk along the waterfront," Ethan urged, hopefully. He couldn't let her go. Not yet. Not ever.

She nodded, her smile soft and sweet, and accepted the hand he held out to her. They walked in silence, stopping at a small park to lean against the railing and stare out at the water and beyond.

Lauren turned to him, studying him. "You never talked about your family because you probably didn't want to tip your hand. Tell me about them now. What makes you who you are?"

Her question surprised him, but he was more than happy to accommodate her. Thinking about his family made him smile. "I'm one of the lucky ones. I have great parents. My dad, despite his many business ventures, always made time for us. My mother immersed herself in her charities and volunteering. We've all been instilled with a sense of duty to this community. We give back any way we can. As kids, we spent every Christmas day dishing up dinner at the homeless shelter, and that was only one of the many things we did." He found himself telling her about his childhood, the boating excursions throughout Puget Sound and Canada, the family dinners his mother insisted on, the many ways they helped out in the community, and their long history in Seattle.

"Your family sounds incredible."

"They are, which makes it hard to measure up. They have high expectations for all of us. I spent the first ten years of my adult life increasing the family fortune. But my family's legacy has always been to give back to the community. This is how I'm giving back." He turned to her, holding both her hands to his heart. "With the gift of hockey."

"You think this community will embrace hockey?" She stared into his eyes, her own hazel eyes large and oddly proud.

"Absolutely. Don't you?"

She chewed on that for a moment and nodded, almost reluctantly. "I think so."

"I'll do my damnedest to help that along. I'm starting youth hockey camps next year and programs at the local rinks for kids who can't afford hockey gear and lessons. We'll be entrenched in the league's charity causes along with a few of our own. We're partnering with Seattle's football and baseball teams, along with the women's pro basketball team, in various charity programs."

"You seem to have it all figured out."

"This was in the works long before I purchased the team. Once I made a deal with the Sleezers, there was no turning back no matter how badly I felt. I'd made the commitment, I'd see it through."

She didn't answer, just turned away and stared out at the water, her hands gripping the railing. He wondered if she was regretting her decision to leave.

"So where do you go now that the draft is over?" he asked.

"I don't know. I'm not sure."

"Are you heading back to Gainesville?"

"The team is gone, there's nothing there for me."

"If you need more money or—"

"I have plenty. You've been more than generous."

"I just—"

"—don't want me to sue you?" she finished for him, her words shocking him to the core.

"Who told you about that?"

"Not important. You should know me well enough to know I'd never do such a thing."

"I never thought you would."

"I'm sorry about what happened to you, Ethan."

"It's not like I make a habit out of dating employees. I'm just so busy, unfortunately, that's the only place I seem to meet decent women."

"You might want to be more careful in the future."

Right now he couldn't imagine his future without Lauren, but he couldn't ask her to stay knowing they couldn't keep their hands off each other.

There was only one way to handle this which made sense, yet made no sense. Even worse, Brad had come up with the idea, and Brad's ideas were way out in left field to say the least. But he couldn't lose her. Desperation poured over him, engulfing him with the fear he was on the verge of losing her forever. Desperate times, desperate measures.

He took the leap. The words came out in a rush of uncharacteristic insecurity. "I want you to stay, Lauren."

"You know that's not possible."

"What if I make it possible, make it something which didn't mess with either of our reputations?"

"How the hell would you do that? You're good, Ethan, but you're not that good."

Ethan put his hands on her shoulders and turned her back to face him again. He rested his hands on her waist, and stared deeply into her hazel eyes, which were decidedly green right now.

"Marry me, Lauren." He spoke with absolute conviction.

"Marry you?" Her mouth dropped open, she staggered back a step, and stopped by the railing behind her. He steadied her.

"Yes. Marry me."

"So we can continue to work together? Ethan, how much have you had to drink?"

"Only that bottle of wine I shared with you tonight. I've never been more sober. Together you and I can build something special in this city." He liked Brad's insane idea more and more so he ran with it.

"You're proposing we get married so we can be business partners?" She shook her head and laughed, as if he'd lost his mind. So maybe he had. Over her.

He snorted. "Hardly. Though there'd be that, too. We'd be partners in life."

She slipped away from him, hugging herself. "I can't."

"Why not? Take a leap of faith."

"Faith? This from a man who misrepresented himself from day one."

"I was as honest with you as I could be. I'm so sorry, Lauren. If I could've handled it any other way, I would have."

Lauren shook her head over and over as tears filled her eyes and ran down her cheeks. "I need to go, Ethan. You've started a good thing here. Good luck." She ran toward her car. Her heels clicked on the sidewalk in a frenzied beat to escape from him.

Ethan sprinted after her. "Lauren, don't go. Please." They were almost back to the parking lot, and panic clawed at his insides.

She turned to him. "I can't stay." Through her tears, he saw the pure agony in her eyes, as if she wished things could be different. Things could be different. He'd show her. He would. If only she'd stay.

She unlocked her car with her key fob and reached for the door. He held it shut with his hand.

"Ethan. Please," she implored him.

He stared into her eyes, and the truth hit him like a lightning bolt streaking across Puget Sound on a stormy day.

He loved her.

He loved her.

"Marry me, Lauren. Please. I can't see my life without you in it."

"Don't make it any worse." More tears flowed down her cheeks, and he stepped forward to wipe them with the pad of his thumb.

"I love you, Lauren." There he'd said it. The truth. Words he'd never uttered to another woman not part of his family.

Her eyes shot wide open at the word *love*. "You—you can't mean that. You can't."

"I do." He spoke with bone-deep certainty.

She swallowed and shook her head. "I have to go."

"Stay. Be my wife. We'll build a hockey legacy together and

raise little hockey players and good citizens."

She shook her head, as one final lone tear painted her cheek. The decisiveness in her gaze wrote their final chapter.

Hesitating briefly, he stepped back and allowed her to open the car door.

She got in and looked up at him with hazel eyes full of sorrow. "I'm sorry. I can't do it. Can't go through this again."

"I'm not Max."

"I know. I'm sorry. I can't."

"Lauren, I love you," he pleaded, sounding so pathetic and desperate he didn't recognize his own voice.

"No, it's over."

Jesus, he'd bared his soul, and she'd treated it like an appetizer. When a man hit rock bottom, he had one thing left to hang onto—his pride. Ethan gathered his around him like a Kevlar vest and hardened his expression. "I was wrong about you—about us—if you think for one moment I would do to you what Max did."

"But you already did, Ethan. Don't you see? Maybe you didn't cheat on me with women but you cheated on my heart by not trusting me with the truth."

She shut the door and mouthed goodbye as she backed out of her parking space.

Ethan stood on the pavement and watched his future shot at happiness drive away. He didn't know how long he stood there. When the first drops of rain hit his cheeks, he trudged toward his car. It hadn't rained in Seattle since Lauren had arrived. How fitting it rained now that she was leaving and taking his heart with her.

Chapter 18—Penalty Kill

Lauren turned off her cell, her computer, her wireless, her tablet, and all the lights in her Seattle apartment. She curled into a little ball on the couch, wallowed in self-pity, and alternated between sobbing hysterically and staring blindly at old movies all night. Even Horace couldn't console her though he gave it his best shot by purring so loudly she had to crank the volume on the TV. Her eyes were swollen from crying. Her throat scratchy from sobbing. Her heart leaden with despair.

She spent two days like that. Tomorrow she'd pull herself up by her laces and get back on the ice, starting with contacting several the minor league teams.

Ethan said he loved her.

He couldn't mean it. It was just another ploy to convince her to stay.

Sometime during the night she fell into an exhausted sleep and woke to someone pounding on her door. Startled awake, she shot to a sitting position, glancing at the clock on the wall. It was past noon. She'd slept most of the morning away. She hurried to the door before the person on the other side had the neighbors calling 911, glancing at the wall mirror on the way by. Big mistake. She looked like crap with her puffy cheeks, red eyes, and wild, tangled hair. As if it would help, Lauren smoothed back her hair and gathered her composure, peeking out a side window. Her aunt stood in front of the door wearing a formidable frown.

Damn.

Reluctantly, she opened the door. Aunt Jo and her dad stood there. Lauren never expected to be double-teamed, especially when she wasn't sure what game they were playing.

Her aunt walked in the door with a smirk on her face, obviously pleased with herself, while her father slinked along behind, as if ashamed. Aunt Jo must have kicked some major Schneider ass, not that Lauren had a clue why, but Aunt Jo rarely needed a reason to put her brother in his place.

Her aunt's smirk disappeared as she eyed Lauren's face. "What happened to you?"

"I have a cold, and I fell asleep on the couch."

Her aunt tilted her head and gave her the *eye*, the one usually reserved for Lauren's brothers when they'd been bad, or Aunt Jo had caught them in a lie, or both. Much to Lauren's surprise, her aunt didn't push the issue. Whatever Aunt Jo's mission for being there, she didn't lose focus.

Lauren brewed a pot of coffee and poured three cups, while her father and aunt sat down on the couch. After serving the coffee, Lauren stood across from them, suspicious of their intentions.

"So Dad, what brings you to Seattle?" As furious as he'd been over the move, she never expected him to set foot in the city and assumed he would quit the team.

He mumbled something, not meeting her eyes.

"What?"

"Free agent and scouting stuff."

"So you're still working for the Gi—Sockeyes?"

He didn't answer but Aunt Jo nudged him with a sharp elbow and he grunted. "I'm keeping the job. Parker made me an offer I couldn't refuse."

Her father was staying after all he said about Ethan? She rubbed her eyes and took a long gulp of coffee.

"We think you should stay, too, honey. This is a great opportunity. Don't we, Lon?"

He nodded and finally met Lauren's gaze. "I was wrong, Lauren. Wrong to be mad at you for doing your job. Pro sports teams are shook up all the time. The Giants' upper management had become complacent. They weren't interested in trying different things to see what worked, and they'd surrounded themselves with a coaching staff mired in mediocrity. I still don't like the move, but— and I never thought I'd admit this—Seattle is going to be a great hockey town. I just know it."

"And that's why you're staying on?" He was right, and Lauren knew it. Sure, it still hurt when she recalled the charities the Giants had served and the great people she'd met, but the team had moved on, and so would she.

"I'm staying because it's the right thing to do, and I want to be part of this great legacy we're building here. Don't you?"

She stared at him and blinked several times, not believing her ears. "It doesn't matter what I want. I can't have it." Lauren sniffled and rubbed her eyes.

Her aunt snorted. "Don't be so short-sighted. Of course, you can have it."

"I can't. Not after how Ethan lied to me. I trusted a man once, and he took my trust and exploited it all the way to divorce court. I don't know Ethan half as well as I knew Max and look how wrong I was about Max."

"Ethan's not Max," her father said, shocking the hell out of her.

Lauren had to sit down because she was certain the end of the world was on the horizon. "You're defending Ethan?"

"Crazy, huh?" Her dad smiled, and Lauren had to smile, too.

Aunt Jo jabbed him in the ribs again and his smile flipped upside down with annoyance. "Tell her. Tell her what you heard. *Now.*" Not even her father stood up to Aunt Jo when she used her badass voice.

Her father swallowed. "I should've told you this sooner, but I was still angry and bitter my group didn't get the team. Come to find out they were never really in the running."

"Tell me what?"

"Ethan didn't have a choice but to lie to you—to all of us."

"Everyone has a choice." She'd been sucked into some weird vortex where her father and Ethan weren't at odds but were on the same page.

"No. Not Ethan. Not if he wanted the team. I have it from a good source the league placed a gag order on him until the season ended. If the truth got out, the deal was off."

Lauren put her hand up to her mouth. "Are you serious?"

"Dead serious. Yes, he deceived us, but I can tell you for a fact deception wasn't his first choice or the way he would've handled the situation if it were in his power."

Lauren sat up straighter and stiffened, as she attempted to process this information. Ethan was a man of his word, and he'd agreed to keep the sale a secret. How did a man with principles deal with a situation forcing him to hide the truth. Doing so must have destroyed him on some level, and she'd done the rest.

"I don't see how this changes anything." Deep down she wasn't as certain.

Her father sighed. "I guess it's your prerogative to make that determination. It changed things for me. That and opening my eyes to the good things he's doing here."

Lauren hugged her stomach. She felt sick, like she might pass out or need to run for the bathroom.

Ethan had said he loved her.

She tried to harden her heart and resist the conflicting emotions slamming against each other, making her dizzy and confused. Ethan wasn't the first man who'd told her that, and she'd been dumb enough to believe the first guy.

But Ethan wasn't Max. He was Ethan. Even her father agreed.

God, her head hurt. Big time. Like someone had rolled over it with a semi.

He loved her. He wanted to marry her.

"He proposed to me as a way to keep me here," she murmured more to herself than her family. "He said he loved me."

A hushed silence filled the room until it was deafening. Even Horace, lounging on her father's lap, stopped purring.

"Do you love him?" Aunt Jo recovered first, while Lon merely stared out the window.

Lauren mulled over the words in her mind, tested them, tried them on for size. She'd told Max she loved him, and she had in her own way, but it had been a desperate, needy, immature love, instead of a love bound by mutual respect, trust, and shared goals. She had two out of three with Ethan; did she have the third? Could she trust him?

"Do you love him?" her aunt prodded.

"I think so," she admitted.

"You *think* so?" Her father turned to her. "That's a bit indecisive."

"Yes, yes, I do." Lauren let her heart speak for her.

Her aunt, the gay romantic, grinned at her. "Go to him. Tell him you changed your mind."

She looked to her father, who nodded. "You two are a good pair. On and off the ice. A person doesn't get too many chances in life for a relationship like that. You'll be the most powerful hockey couple in the league."

She didn't give a damn about power. She gave a damn about Ethan, his hopes, his dreams, his smile, his lean, ripped body, his clever comebacks. All of it. Even his drive and ambition and infuriatingly single-minded focus. Ethan, the man she'd thrown in jail without the benefit of a trial. She'd been a self-centered bitch never considering what he'd gone through to get this team. Now she understood. He hurt as much as she did. Damn it, she'd see to it she never hurt him again if his offer was still good.

"I need to find him. Now."

But first she needed a shower.

* * * *

Ethan rubbed his eyes and sat back in his chair. The salary cap numbers swam on the monitor in front of him. He stood, stretching his cramped muscles. He'd been sitting too long, and it was late.

The last month had been nuts for the management of a new hockey team. Ethan should've been prepared, yet he wasn't. Not really. It started with the player buyout period, free agent talks, the draft, and free agency. It hit with speed of the Indy 500, and at times Ethan felt he and his staff were driving round in circles as they plotted and planned for next season and beyond.

He dived in with the enthusiasm he was famous for—not a hands-off owner in any way, shape, or form. He showed up early and left late, spending time at his other office during the middle of the day doing his *normal* job for Parker Corp., while doing the job he was passionate about before and after.

He'd always been a businessman first, with a single-minded purpose toward his goal to the exclusion of all else. Not this time. You'd think a man with so much on his plate wouldn't be pining for a woman when he'd never been in an official, committed relationship with her.

It'd been damn hard to get Lauren out of his head when he'd seen her every second of every day. It was even harder when he didn't see her at all.

Today marked the third day since Lauren had left the team. He ached to touch her, to sweep her up in his arms like some Disney hero, and carry her away to a place where only they mattered. He'd cracked open the armor around his heart and told her he loved her. In return she'd walked away and never looked back, with not so much as one word from her in three fucking days.

"Ethan?"

He turned at the sound of Kaley's voice. "Yes?"

"Here are the drafts of the promotional materials the marketing team put together. You said you wanted to see them."

"Great, just put them on the desk." He turned his back to her, looking across the parking lot to the partially finished hockey arena, their pride and joy. He felt Kaley's eyes drilling into his back. Why didn't she leave?

He turned with a long-suffering sigh. "Is there something else?" He forced patience into his voice.

"You're just going to let her walk away?" Kaley's eyes narrowed, and she shot him a glare that would've withered a lesser man.

"It's her choice, not mine. I'd love to keep her on staff."

"That's not what I'm talking about."

Ethan gingerly stepped into that mine field known as discussing his personal life at work—something he rarely, if ever, did. "Then what are you talking about?" Sometimes playing the dense male definitely helped.

"Lauren and you. Your personal relationship."

"Oh." No use denying it. She was Lauren's best friend and most likely knew every detail. "Not a good idea since I'm her boss."

"Because you've been burned before?"

That asshole Brad. Was nothing sacred with that big-mouthed bastard?

"Something like that. We both stand to lose too much by having an affair. Besides, she's not one to forgive easily."

"Do you have any idea why that is, Ethan?"

"Not completely. I know she's divorced from a former player turned minor-league coach."

"Then you don't know why what you did hurt as much as his lying, cheating, and gambling hurt her. She married him on a whim, a totally out of character whim, because he was the first guy she'd ever truly fallen in love with. As a result, she lost her job with the Giants. A few months later they traded him. She moved with him. He took her blind trust and inexperience in relationships and used it against her to his advantage. When the team went on the road, he had a puck bunny or two, or three, every night. He spent money on women, booze, and gambling at an alarming rate, especially on a rookie salary. Lauren didn't know. He'd insisted on handling all the finances. When he quit coming home or answering her calls, she still made excuses, until she surprised on his birthday in his hotel room while he was entertaining three puck bunnies. He left her with a mountain of debt she's been digging out of ever since. Her father convinced the Giants to hire her back in a clerical role, and she scrambled her way up the ladder. But trust a man in a committed relationship? No, she hasn't done that in years."

"I had no idea about the details." Ethan understood all too much about trust. He didn't trust much himself. When people fell short of his expectations, he quit taking them at face value, except for his family and a few lifelong friends.

"Well, now you do."

"I don't see what it changes. Two people with serious trust issues don't make for a good combination."

"You don't trust Lauren?"

"She doesn't trust me. I told her I loved her. That I wanted to marry her." He blurted out the truth, hearing the stark pain in his voice.

Kaley didn't blink, not even slightly surprised by his admission. "Max never fought for her. Why don't you fight for her?"

"I tried. It's too late."

"When you were told time and time again that you couldn't get a team, couldn't get the zoning for the arena, and Seattle wasn't a hockey town, did you accept what they said, or fight to prove them wrong?"

"I fought to prove them wrong." Ethan knew where this was going.

"Why don't you fight to prove Lauren wrong?"

"I can't leave town right now. Not with the team in the middle of free-agent negotiations."

"What if I told you a secret?" Kaley glanced around as if the walls had ears.

"A secret?"

"Lauren's still here. She didn't have anywhere to go, and she's developed an affinity for Seattle."

"She's still here?"

"She sure is." Kaley's smug smile should've pissed him off, but it didn't.

She's still here. Lauren hasn't left. Ethan needed a plan, a way to woo her back, convince her he was a man she could depend on. He considered his options for all of two seconds.

Screw the plan.

He grabbed his phone and iPad and sprinted for the door, ignoring Mina's annoyance or how people cleared out of his way as he ran past. The elevator took too long, so he crashed down the stairwell, three steps at a time, and ran for his car. Tires squealed as he sped out of the parking lot and into the blinding sun of a Seattle summer day.

Chapter 19—The Top Shelf

Lauren wasn't at home. Ethan tried her cell. Nothing. Called Kaley. She didn't answer. He called Lon. Again nothing. Didn't anyone ever answer his or her phone? He sat in his car for a few hours in front of her apartment complex and finally got out, wondering if she'd left the door unlocked, and he could wait inside, but it was locked.

He paced in front of her door until her neighbor, some scrawny, old guy came out of his apartment a few doors down, hands on hips, and glared at him. The guy walked closer and confronted Ethan.

"You have business with her?"

"Uh, yeah, I do."

"Well, she ain't home. That's pretty obvious."

"Do you know where she went?"

"If I did, I wouldn't tell you." He pulled out his cell phone. "Why don't you move along before I call the cops?"

"Do I look like a burglar?" He pointed at his expensive sports car sitting in the driveway.

"How in hell l do I know? You could've stolen the thing. Now move along."

With a sigh, Ethan left reluctantly. He'd texted Lauren and left messages on her phone.

If she didn't call back, he'd find a way to reach her. He had to. He couldn't wait one more night, and obviously he couldn't wait in front of her house, not with her ancient neighbor standing guard. Feeling defeated, he drove home to his big empty house on Queen Anne Hill overlooking Puget Sound.

He tried to calm down. Take it easy. There was always tomorrow. But what if right this minute she was accepting a job with another team, looking for a place to live on the East Coast, and paying someone to move her things so she'd never have to come back?

She'd hadn't wanted to live in Seattle, yet Kaley said the city was growing on her.

Defeated, he pulled into his driveway, winding through a clump of old cedars until his old mansion loomed in the near darkness, black, empty, and looking as lonely as he felt.

Fight for her.

Kaley's words haunted him. God, he would if he could find her. With all his money, he could put a team of PIs on it, and they'd track her down.

That wasn't the point. That wasn't fighting for her. That was paying someone else to do the fighting, and it wouldn't mean as much to him or to her. He had to do this on his own. Do the research, do the legwork, do the detail stuff he hated because he was doing it for her.

Lauren.

The woman who'd stolen his heart so subtly he hadn't realized it until a few days ago. He loved her more than he'd ever thought possible, with every molecule bouncing around in his body, with every bit of oxygen left in his lungs, with every dream he'd ever dreamed. She melted the ice in his heart and made the sun shine on the rainiest Seattle day.

He loved her.

And dammit to hell, he wasn't letting her go.

Ethan slowed his car and squinted into the darkness. Someone sat on his doorstep, hugging herself with her arms, and rocking back and forth as if cold.

Fucking hell.

At first he couldn't believe what he was seeing, certain it was an illusion drawn by a desperate man so completely out of his league in his current situation. He stopped next to the front walkway and got out. When she stood and faced him, still hugging herself, her eyes full of uncertainty, and her lips quivering, he knew they both wanted the same thing.

He walked within six feet from her, drinking her in, loving her tentative yet determined smile.

"Lauren."

"Ethan." She stared into his eyes. Her uncertainty slowly replaced by a glint of determination.

He took the steps two at a time and halted in front of her. "You're here."

"Damn right. Where the hell have you been?" she chastised him with a teasing smile. He grinned back, unable to stop himself.

"Looking to hell and back for you."

"I've been here for hours."

"I've been looking for you for hours. Why didn't you call?"

"I left my cell in my apartment. It was dead anyway."

"Ahhh, crap."

She just shrugged and looked around. "You have a beautiful house. A mansion, really. You live here by yourself?"

The change of subject caught him off guard. He nodded, finding it hard to believe they were discussing houses when all he wanted to do was take her in his arms and kiss the hell out of her and make her promise to never leave him again. "Yes, it's old, built by my ancestors."

Unable to bear their polite conversation any longer, he wrapped her in his arms and crushed her to him. She hugged him back and pulled his head down for a scorching kiss which kicked time on its ass and froze the world around them.

Heaven only knew how long they stood there, kissing.

Finally he set her back at arm's length. "Come inside. Let's talk."

And more than that, because now that he'd gotten her back, he wasn't letting her go.

* * * *

Lauren followed Ethan inside a cavernous, historical mansion that should've been cold and foreboding but was decorated in country colors giving it a warm, cozy feel despite its size.

They walked into a kitchen big enough to serve dinner for the entire team. She took the glass of wine he offered as he grasped her free hand and led her outside to a patio that ran the width of the house with views as breathtaking as a house like this deserved.

"This is incredible. This entire place. How long have you lived here?"

"Forever. My great, great, great grandfather built it. When my parents decided to downsize a few years ago, I snatched it up."

"You live here all by yourself?" She stared in amazement at the manicured lawns and proud, old trees, all framing a scenic view of Puget Sound, glittering in fading orange glow from a sunset over the distant Olympic Mountains. She hadn't known God made views like this. Obviously, He did.

Ethan raised one eyebrow as if she'd asked a silly question.

"I know, you have people who take care of everything," she

teased. "This view is epic, beyond anything I could ever imagine."

He nodded. "I don't want to talk about this house, except to ask when you're moving in."

"What *do* you want to talk about?" She skirted around his remark.

"You saying yes." Straight and to the point. He didn't make her suffer just to watch her squirm.

She considered yanking his chain for sheer orneriness, but didn't have the heart. "Yes."

"What did you say?" His blue eyes grew troubled, as if he were waiting for a 'but.'

"I said yes," she repeated, unable to stop the smile spreading across her face.

"Yes? You're saying yes?"

She nodded and held her wine glass up for a toast. He clinked his to hers and a second later smothered her in his arms, while wine drizzled down their backsides to puddle on the patio.

"I love you, Lauren," he whispered against her lips. His sexy grin melted any residual doubt of the truth behind his words.

She drew back, needing to see the look on his face, a powerful combination of love and passion. "I love you, too."

"Do you think we can make it?"

"Do you think the Sockeyes can?" she shot back.

He blinked a few times, as if not getting the connection. "Uh, yeah, absolutely. How can they miss with the two of us guiding the way?"

"Exactly. And how can we miss?"

"We can't. I just hope you can learn to trust me." Concern filled his gaze.

"I already do, honey. I do. I know about the gag order."

"Who told you that?" His eyes narrowed for a moment, but he was obviously too happy to stay annoyed for too long. His grin came back full force, lighting up his eyes from his heart outward.

"A most unlikely supporter. My dad."

"Your dad?"

She nodded. "With a hockey legend like him on our side, how can we go wrong?"

"We can't go wrong, even without him on our side."

She hugged him close, buried her face in his chest, and breathed in his scent, looking forward to her future—their future. It wouldn't be easy, not with the team resistance led by Cooper, the staff thinking she'd seduced Ethan or vice versa, and the challenge of living with a stubborn man, but hell she was one stubborn woman.

Besides, they had love on their side.

Together they'd conquer any challenge on the ice or off, raise little hockey players who were also good citizens, hoist the Cup a time or two, hopefully more, and make a lifetime of memories together in a beautiful city which was now her home.

~ THE END ~

Thank you for spending time in my world. I hope you enjoyed reading this book. If you did, please help other readers discover this book by leaving a review.

For news on upcoming Jami Davenport books, sign up for my newsletter by clicking here.

Did you find any errors? Please email me so I may correct them and upload a new version. You can reach me via the contact page on my website: http://www.jamidavenport.com/contact/

~ THE END ~

Thank you for spending time in my world. I hope you enjoyed reading this book. If you did, please help other readers discover this book by leaving a review.

COMPLETE BOOKLIST

The following Jami Davenport titles are available in electronic and some are available in trade paperback format.

Madrona Island Series
Madrona Sunset

Evergreen Dynasty Series
Save the Last Dance
Who's Been Sleeping in My Bed?
The Gift Horse

Game On in Seattle—Seattle Sockeyes Hockey
Skating on Thin Ice
Crashing the Boards
Crashing the Net
Love at First Snow
Melting Ice
Blindsided
Hearts on Ice
Bodychecking (Early 2016)

Seattle Lumberjacks Football Series
Fourth and Goal
Forward Passes
Down by Contact
Backfield in Motion
Time of Possession
Roughing the Passer

Standalone Books
Christmas Break

ABOUT THE AUTHOR

If you'd like to be notified of new releases, special sales, and contests, subscribe here: **http://eepurl.com/LpfaL**

USA Today Bestselling Author Jami Davenport writes sexy contemporary and sports romances, including her two new indie endeavors: the Game On in Seattle Series and the Madrona Island Series. Jami's new releases consistently rank in the top fifty on the sports romance and sports genre lists on Amazon, and she has hit the Amazon top hundred authors list in both contemporary romance and genre fiction multiple times.

Jami lives on a small farm near Puget Sound with her Green Beret-turned-plumber husband, a Newfoundland cross with a tennis ball fetish, a prince disguised as an orange tabby cat, and an opinionated Hanoverian mare.

Jami works in IT for her day job and is a former high school business teacher. She's a lifetime Seahawks and Mariners fan and is waiting for the day professional hockey comes to Seattle. An avid boater, Jami has spent countless hours in the San Juan Islands, a common setting in her books. In her opinion, it's the most beautiful place on earth.

Website: http://www.jamidavenport.com
Events Blog: http://jamidavenport.blogspot.com
Romancing the Jock Blog: http://www.romancingthejock.com
Twitter Address: @jamidavenport
Facebook: http://www.facebook.com/jamidavenport
Facebook Fan Page:
      http://www.facebook.com/jamidavenportauthor
Pinterest: http://pinterest.com/jamidavenport/
Goodreads:
http://www.goodreads.com/author/show/1637218.Jami_Davenport

Made in the USA
Middletown, DE
14 November 2015